"I'm ready to call the parson right now."

Lauren thought Matt was kidding. "You're still making fun of me."

"Not true." Matt smiled. "If I'd had any sense I would have pounced on the idea the minute I saw you. If we get busy, you could be in the maternity ward not long after your sisters-in-law."

Lauren's cheeks blazed. "You're contemptible! Let's go back into the house."

"Not yet." Matt trailed his finger down her cheek. She glanced up with hesitation, sure he was going to kiss her. But he moved away. "I'll pick you up at six."

Lauren was strangely disappointed. "I'm not going out with you," she insisted.

"Well, then. Let's go back in. I have a very interesting story to tell your parents...."

Kate Denton is a pseudonym for the writing team of Carolyn Hake and Jeanie Lambright. Both are Texans by adoption, Carolyn having come from Louisiana, Jeanie from Oklahoma. They work as specialists for the federal government in Health and Handicap Services (Carolyn) and Equal Employment Opportunity (Jeanie). Each has three children, and an assortment of cats and dogs! They are both history buffs and their hobbies include cooking, reading, old movies (Carolyn) and traveling, reading, ballet, and writing country and western song lyrics (Jeanie).

Books by Kate Denton

HARLEQUIN ROMANCE
2870—WINNER TAKE ALL

A Business Arrangement

Kate Denton

Harlequin Books

TORONTO • NEW YORK • LONDON
AMSTERDAM • PARIS • SYDNEY • HAMBURG
STOCKHOLM • ATHENS • TOKYO • MILAN

ISBN 0-373-02966-7

Harlequin Romance first edition March 1989

CHAPTER ONE

LAUREN GRAYSON shifted uncomfortably in the armchair and glanced at her watch. Only two minutes had passed since she'd last checked the time. She sighed. Maybe she shouldn't have come. Was it possible to back out now? No, not really.

She was sitting in the reception area of the office of Matthew Kennerly, attorney-at-law, and being subjected every now and then to the not-so-subtle scrutiny of the counselor's secretary. Soft music played in the background as the efficient-looking woman typed on a word processor and glanced frequently in Lauren's direction. *She definitely knows,* Lauren thought.

Lauren had made the appointment the day before.

"And the nature of your business?" the secretary had asked.

"Just tell him I'm calling about the newspaper ad. He'll understand."

"Oh, yes. Hold on while I check his calendar."

Lauren had been surprised. Apparently he'd discussed the situation with this woman, because she scheduled an appointment for Lauren quite matter-of-factly.

"Can you come in at nine tomorrow morning, Ms Grayson?"

It had been as simple as that. Except now that the interview was at hand, Lauren's cool demeanor was fading. Her palms were moist as she adjusted the hem of her pink linen skirt to cover the tops of her knees. Her throat felt constricted. Just how was she going to handle this? In a businesslike manner, she reminded herself. Just as she'd planned.

But all thoughts of business began to fade when the door leading into the reception area opened and Matthew Kennerly appeared. Until that moment, she'd had an image in her mind of the man who'd answered her advertisement. Lauren had visualized someone older—a three-piece suit, graying-at-the-temples type. Matthew Kennerly definitely didn't fit her expectations.

Lauren was taken aback. Was his successful practice based solely on his reputation as one of Dallas's sharpest divorce lawyers, she wondered, or could it also be due to the fact he happened to be devastatingly handsome?

She thought of some of the men who were constantly on the list of the ten most desirable males in America—the movie and television stars. In Lauren's opinion none of them could hold a candle to Matthew Kennerly. He wore a white dress shirt, sleeves rolled to the elbow, tie loosened at the neck. His hair was dark, almost a blue-black, his skin tanned a golden bronze. Pale gray eyes, with thick, dark eyelashes, looked at her with a mischievous twinkle. He stood about five foot eleven—not short but not too tall, either. Wearing heels, she could fit quite easily in his arms, Lauren mused, her mind conjuring up a vision of the two of them entwined on a dance floor.

"Well, do I pass inspection?" he said, smiling, clearly amused at the once-over he was receiving.

Lauren could feel the flush of her embarrassment. She hadn't meant to be so obvious. She was getting ahead of herself—and forgetting her primary objective. But he wasn't what she had expected—not at all. Despite her discomfort, she managed to reply evenly, "Sorry. I didn't mean to be rude." She rose from her chair and held out her hand. "I'm Lauren Grayson."

"Well, Lauren Grayson," he drawled, "come on into my office and we'll talk. I don't have much time. I'm on a tight schedule today."

Lauren followed him through the door. The office was big, with bookshelves lining two walls and floor-to-ceiling windows giving a spectacular view of the Hyatt Regency to the left and a hint of Fort Worth off in the distance. Lauren's trained eye told her the decorating had been done by an experienced designer. The balance of colors— browns and tans and dark blues, and the choice of furniture were impeccable. There was an order to everything, with the exception of the massive oak desk, which was littered with files and papers.

Matt Kennerly motioned her to sit on the couch and he took one of the two side chairs.

"Well," she said, "I guess there are a lot of questions you want to ask me."

"A few. Mostly basic stuff."

"Fine." Lauren straightened against the back of the couch. "What would you like to know first?"

"Do you type?"

"I beg your pardon?"

"Do you type?" He noticed the surprised look on her face. "Lord, no—" his hand slapped his forehead "—might have known. I guess you don't make coffee, either."

"Instant. But does it matter?"

"Well, of course it matters—or did you just expect to sit around and look pretty?" As if responding to his own question, his eyes took in Lauren, moving slowly from her shoulder-length, chestnut-brown hair to her dark brown eyes, then wandering down her slender, curvaceous body to her long, shapely legs. Was this the man who, only minutes before, had chided her for looking him over? "Well, do I pass inspection?" she parroted his earlier words.

"Definitely." He got up and walked over to the window. "I suppose you want to talk about salary and income?"

"Not necessarily. Money isn't a major consideration. At least not for me."

"That's unusual. It's the first thing most people want to talk about."

Lauren was surprised. He certainly didn't beat around the bush, but then lawyers generally made a habit of getting straight to the point, she thought. He probably knew more about this kind of thing than she did. But she certainly didn't want his money. She didn't need his money. She had plenty of her own.

"Okay." He nodded his head as though he'd come to some sort of understanding with himself. "You obviously haven't been through this routine before. Is this your first interview?"

"Yes," Lauren admitted, again taken aback by his directness.

"Well, I'm willing to take a chance. When can you be available?"

Not only was this man direct, he was decisive. "Anytime," she said, glad everything was finally going smoothly. "I'd like to get acquainted as soon as possible. How about tonight? Or, if you're busy, tomorrow night would be okay."

"Tonight or tomorrow night? This is getting interesting." He moved from the window to the desk. "I'd been thinking about something during the day myself." He pulled out the executive swivel chair and sat down. "Just what did *you* have in mind?"

"Dinner. Drinks, maybe. Then some time getting to know each other."

"Hmm. Your employment history must be interesting reading, Ms Grayson." He raised one eyebrow. "But I'm afraid what I have in mind is all business."

Lauren was growing increasingly uncomfortable. What did he think—that everything was going to be handled on paper? Business arrangement aside, even she hadn't visualized a relationship with no personal touch.

"Look," he said, shaking his head, "I guess I was just hoping for a few extras. But they're not essential. Forget the typing and coffee. As long as you can get along with the public, and with me, that'll be fine. I'll also expect punctuality, professionalism and a good disposition."

"What are you talking about? We seem to be on totally different wavelengths. Are you making fun of me?"

"I'm not trying to," he answered. "But I'm beginning to wonder whether this could possibly work out. I need a receptionist who takes her job seriously."

"Receptionist? Is that what this is all about?" A smile crossed Lauren's face. "You seem to have your appointments mixed up, Mr. Kennerly. I'm not here about a job." She pulled a piece of paper from her purse, unfolded it and handed it to him. "I'm here about this."

Matt Kennerly looked shocked as he read the brief message. It was a photocopy of the advertisement Lauren had recently placed in the "personal" column of *The Dallas Sentinel*:

PARTNER WANTED. Tired of the singles scene? Looking for that special someone to start a home and family with? Single career woman, 29, seeks re-

sponsible male for businesslike marriage. Respond
to P.O. Box 3WX8, Dallas, TX 75239

Stapled to the sheet of paper was one of Matthew
Kennerly's business cards.

"I'm afraid I don't understand," he said, placing the
paper in the middle of his desk. He did look puzzled,
Lauren decided, as he leaned forward in his swivel chair,
his eyes scanning the ad, then his head shaking as though
in disbelief.

Lauren walked over to the front of the desk. "That
arrived in the mail yesterday—a response to my advertisement. I called and made an appointment with your
secretary so we could meet face-to-face to discuss the
possibility. You know, an interview."

"You put *this* in the newspaper?" He picked up the
paper and waved it in her direction.

Lauren nodded.

"Lady, you've got to be kidding."

"I don't really think it's a matter to kid about, do
you?"

"I damn sure don't."

"So we agree."

"Well then, now that we agree," he said, "I'd like an
explanation." His eyes, suddenly a steely gray, studied
her.

Lauren turned from the desk and walked across the
room. She stared at a painting on the wall, a watercolor
of Texas bluebonnets. She felt the heat of embarrassment on her face. Despite the little speech she had re-
hearsed earlier, despite the numerous conversations she'd
had with herself about what she'd say in an "interview," she was momentarily at a loss for words. But
surely the man was interested in her proposal—he

wouldn't have answered the ad if he wasn't. So why was he having trouble understanding it?

"I have a very busy career," she began, turning toward him.

He smiled. "Just what is it that you do—other than placing advertisements?"

Lauren wasn't amused. "I'm an interior decorator."

"I see." He bowed his head, but in what, a nod of dismissal? Boredom? Why wasn't he being more helpful, more agreeable? After all, he'd responded to her ad, she told herself again. Even though he was sitting and she was standing, Lauren felt as if she were in the witness box.

"My business is successful," she continued, "and it keeps me very busy. But I want more out of life. I think a lot of people do." This was the pat speech she'd gone over a thousand times since placing the ad, an attempt to logically explain why she had advertised for a husband. But her credibility seemed to be slipping as rapidly as her confidence.

All her reasons were so clear in her mind. So why was it so difficult to explain them to him? He'd probably think she was odd if she admitted she'd never been in love, and accuse her of being paranoid if she said the men she'd met were shallow and superficial, more interested in her money and her family's social status than in her. She'd never be able to make him understand her feelings that life was passing her by and that she wanted children, a family—and wanted them badly enough that she'd finally decided to settle for less than a great romance, that the time had come to be practical.

She looked across the desk and was captured by his penetrating gray-eyed stare. Would marriage to Matt Kennerly be settling for less? She noticed the dimples that played in his cheeks, the lock of dark hair that fell over his forehead. Something made him seem more, not less. What was happening? Surely she was too mature to get giddy over a man she'd just met.

Lauren had always thought she knew who she was and what she wanted. She was twenty-nine years old. She had a master's degree in art history, a partnership in a budding business, and a standing in the community, as the youngest child of Lyle and Jeanette Grayson—prominent figures in the Dallas establishment.

But she wasn't happy. Not unhappy really, but not content, either. Did she feel lonely? She didn't think so. Yet something was missing from her life....

"So you've decided to advertise for a husband," he prompted. "Then get married, have kids. Just like that?"

"What? Yes. No. Well, I mean...not just like that." He'd caught her off guard. "Naturally, we'd need to get to know each other first. To be sure we're compatible. That we want the same things.

"You see," she continued, "I've come up with a different approach—the sort that works in business. You need an employee, say, or a product so you advertise. Wait for responses. You do interviews, and when you find what you're looking for you negotiate a deal. All clear-cut and businesslike. Only instead of employee or product, it would be marital partner, and instead of deal, it would be marriage license."

One corner of his mouth curved upward. "I must say I've never been approached with anything quite like this before."

"I decided the situation called for drastic measures." She laughed nervously, unsure if he was teasing her or if things were going better between them.

"Drastic measures or not, I'm afraid I'm not interested." He glanced down at his watch. "And I'm really short of time." He got up from the desk as if dismissing her.

"You mean you don't even want to try?"

"You're telling me you're willing to audition?" His lip curled in a sardonic expression.

The intent of his words sank into Lauren's mind. He thought—he believed—Lauren didn't even want to think about it. What kind of impression had she made on him? And what sort of person was he to think such a thing, anyway? "You've got it all wrong."

"No, I don't think so." Matt moved around the desk and came close to her. "Every time I think I've seen and heard everything, something happens that surprises me. I thought I was beyond surprises by now. You—" he pointed his finger at her and nodded "—are a clever one." He reached for her arm.

"Keep your hands off me," she ordered, pulling away from his touch. "I placed that advertisement in good faith and I wanted a serious response. Not some sarcastic lecher with designs about taking advantage of me."

"Good faith! Is this your idea of good faith—making an appointment under false pretenses, trying to run some kind of scam by me, then labeling me a lecher?" He ran his hand through his hair, and shook his head in disbelief. "Now, let's get something straight, very straight. I didn't respond to any tawdry advertisement. You know that, of course, but I'll make the protest just for the sake of argument." He rolled up the sheet of paper and tucked it into the V of Lauren's blouse. "Now you and your little ad can leave the same way you came in."

"But it has your business card stapled to it," Lauren protested, at last admitting to herself that something was badly out of synch.

He sighed in exasperation. "I have those things printed up by the gross. This is either a scam or someone's idea of a sick joke. But I can't believe you, or anyone, would think I'd fall for it."

"But I didn't. It's not what you think."

"Lady, I've heard enough—a damn sight too much. Even if I believed you, and I don't, I'm not the kind of man who would answer a want ad to find a wife—if I wanted a wife. Which I don't."

Matt was face-to-face with her, and Lauren leaned back slightly in an effort to keep her distance. "I don't know what kind of con game you're running, Ms Grayson. Damn, I'm definitely working too hard when I miss such obvious clues as money isn't a consideration." He rolled his eyes to the ceiling. "Is anyone else in on this with you?"

Lauren shook her head. She was speechless. She couldn't believe what was happening.

"Clever one, then, aren't you? But I'm afraid you'll have to look elsewhere for a husband. Tempting as the bait is, I'm not interested. And right now, I've got a stack of evidence and three depositions to go over and I have to be in court in a couple of hours. So I suggest you take your ad and your cute little buns and get out. Consider yourself fortunate I didn't choose to pursue this further."

He opened the office door. "You can expect a bill for my time. I hope you think this little exercise is worth the two hundred bucks you've just blown."

"B-but you've got it all wrong," Lauren stammered, only to receive a look of disbelief in return. "I can see there's been some mistake," she said. "That you knew nothing about this, and that maybe someone's playing a joke. While I personally don't think it's very funny, I'm guessing one of your friends decided it would be a lark." Lauren's head was reeling. She was speaking so rapidly her words were almost running together. Since Matthew Kennerly seemed intent on kicking her out of his office she wanted at least to try to explain. She'd never been in such a humiliating situation in her life.

"Lady, you have an answer for everything, don't you? Well, I repeat, I'm not interested. And I'll also remind you that the meter's still running—your bill just went up another fifty bucks."

The nerve of the man! She'd tried to explain. Any fool could tell they had been the victims of a mistake or a practical joke. Why was he so intent on being aggressively self-righteous? Well, she didn't have to take it. "Just try collecting," Lauren huffed. "You egotistical stuffed shirt—sue me." Lauren could hear his hearty laughter as she slammed the door and made her way out of the office and into the elevator.

"HE WHAT?" Casey bit her lip, in an obvious attempt to stifle the laughter that was threatening to spill out in uncontrollable giggles. Casey, a small red-headed bundle of energy, was as effervescent as champagne, and the cork was about to pop.

"He accused me of being a con artist after his money. At least I think that's what he accused me of—I'm not really too sure. Suffice to say, he doesn't want to try my idea."

Casey surrendered to her urge to laugh, and the sound reverberated in Lauren's ears. "Oh, Lauren—" Casey was unable to continue, as the giggles took over again.

"Talk about adding insult to injury," Lauren grumbled. "Thanks a lot, Casey. You're a big help." As if she needed to subject herself to more ridicule than she'd already endured that morning.

Casey had known about the advertisement and the scheduled meeting with Matthew Kennerly. So when Lauren arrived back at the office, she had been primed to hear the results. When the phone interrupted Lauren's report, Casey had cut the caller short, then leaned her elbows on the glass-topped desk. "Sorry, kiddo. But you must admit, the situation does have its humorous side. Now, let's hear the rest of it—all of it," she said to Lauren.

Lauren dropped into the chair on the opposite side of the desk. She tried to describe what had happened, leaving out some bits here and there. Despite Casey's probing, Lauren wasn't about to give her all the embarrassing details. She prayed no one would ever learn the complete story of what had happened in Matthew Kennerly's office that morning.

When she placed the ad it had never occurred to her that she might be setting herself up for ridicule. Now she couldn't keep from worrying about what Mr. Kennerly might say to the world. Would he find it an amusing tale to tell his friends at the courthouse or in the country club locker room? The thought was mortifying. She could imagine the news spreading all over Dallas; it wouldn't take long to reach her friends and family, and when it did, she'd have to leave town—leave the country. Maybe she could join the army. Did they take women in the French Foreign Legion? "Oooh!" She covered her face with her hands.

"I'm a little surprised by his reaction." Casey's words interrupted Lauren's agonizing. "But then again, he probably thinks you're a crazy woman."

"Crazy? Why crazy? Pick up any newspaper and you'll see. Advertising for relationships is nothing new."

"Relationships are one thing. But a husband and children?" Casey's eyes rolled to the ceiling. "You're lucky the guy wasn't a weirdo or a pervert."

"Well, he may not have been either of those, but I can't think of a single positive thing to say. He was sarcastic, rude, overbearing. And distrustful. He refused to accept my story. For all I know, he really did answer the ad and then lied about it. Maybe he gets some kind of kick out of putting people through the grinder, though it would seem that he has enough chances to do that in the courtroom. Anyway, he had no reason for acting so insulted. You would have thought I'd impugned his honor." She shook her head in angry frustration.

"What does he look like?"

"In a word—gorgeous. Dimples like Robert Redford, sexy full lips like Warren Beatty. But he's got the personality of a scalded warthog."

"Oh, how I would have loved to have been a fly on the wall. I can just imagine it all now." Casey's laughter erupted again.

"I'm beginning to wish I hadn't told you anything about it. I'll never hear the end of this—how you thought it was a bad idea from the word go."

"And I still do." Casey poured herself a cup of coffee. "Your advertisement had all the romance of an old bathrobe, all the allure of washing your hair on a Saturday night. A businesslike approach to your love life? Come off it, Lauren."

"So what's wrong with that? Just how is your love life, Casey?" Lauren's tone was defensive. "How many dates have you had the past six months?"

"Twelve." Casey smiled, a wide Cheshire-cat smile.

"I mean how many successful dates? Let me refresh your memory. It seems I recall one fellow named Bob. Let's see, wasn't he the salesman whose main objectives were to get a meeting with your wealthy uncle and a one-night tumble in your bed?"

"Well, he didn't score—on either count."

"So how about Carlton?"

Casey giggled. "Well, at least he was original. I'd never had a man actually bring his mother on a date before."

Casey's laughter was becoming infectious and Lauren couldn't resist joining in. "What was it she said about you? That you were good stock and she was looking forward to at least five grandchildren?" They both laughed some more. "Shall I continue?"

"Okay, okay, I give up. Your point is well taken," Casey admitted. "But don't you think placing a husband-wanted ad is going a little too far?"

"Drastic circumstances call for drastic measures. Besides, I keep telling you lots of people are using the classifieds these days. Sure there are lots of losers out there, but there have to be some winners, too. It's worth the gamble."

"But couldn't you have made the ad a little more personal, more provocative? Said that you're a gorgeous interior decorator, with long slender gams, big brown eyes, and skin like peaches and cream? That you're looking for a man to settle down with? Preferably one with dimples." Casey sighed. "No, not you. Instead you advertise for a corporate merger."

Lauren frowned. "I think this approach stands a whole lot better chance for success than pitching a line to someone who's only interested in the color of my eyes or what kind of body I've got. And for your information, Miss Know-It-All—" Lauren reached for her purse and opened it "—I checked my post office box again on the way over here and look what I found." Lauren pulled out a couple of envelopes and waved them in the air. "Two more responses to my ad."

Casey looked at her disbelievingly, challengingly. "You mean you're really going to answer another one of those crazy things?"

Actually Lauren's intention in checking the box had been to tear any replies into millions of pieces. But Casey didn't need to know that. Lauren felt as though Casey was issuing a dare she had to accept. A surge of rebellion charged through her.

Lauren had never been one to let a challenge pass. Being the youngest child in her family, she'd learned early in life that challenges usually got her into trouble—especially with two older brothers. But Lauren was stubborn—and impulsive. Then and now. She should have learned her lesson that morning. But she hadn't.

She nodded smugly to Casey and started ripping open one of the envelopes.

"WELL, AREN'T YOU a purty little heifer!" Rex Holley's voice boomed loud enough for the whole of Friday's to hear. Lauren had thought lunch in a busy restaurant would be the best place for them to meet, but she was already regretting her decision as she greeted him at the bar. Rex was a big man—at least six foot four, even without the two-inch heels on the cowboy boots he wore proudly, one ostrich-encased foot propped up on the brass rail.

Lauren made a quick assessment, taking in the plaid western shirt, bolo tie and enormous silver belt buckle resting on a prominent belly. The man was big, huge, in fact. Not only tall like the mighty oak, but just about as wide. Probably weighed three hundred pounds, she thought. She fretted that her hand might be crushed when he shook it in his great paw. But Rex was surprisingly gentle. He took her hand as if it were fine crystal and led her over to a table. "Come sit down, little gal. You want a drink?"

Lauren nodded. She definitely needed a drink. Something strong like a double martini, extra dry. But apparently Rex had his own ideas of what a woman should drink.

"Bring this little lady a champagne cocktail," he said to the waiter, "and a draft for me." He handed Lauren a menu. "Now let's order something good. No pecking around at some dinky little salad. Money's no object."

Lauren skimmed the menu. The waiter had returned with the drinks and was standing over them waiting for their order. Lauren asked for the vegetable medley.

"Now, that wasn't what I meant at all, sweet thing," Rex interceded, changing her order to a large steak. "And a side order of mushrooms." He looked at Lauren, his round weathered face resembling a jack-o'-lantern as his smile spread from ear to ear. "Come on now, tell me all about yourself."

"Well, I'm an interior decorator and—"

"Is that right?" he interrupted. "That's sure a coincidence, cause I used to date one. It was between my first and second marriage. No wait, maybe it was the second and third. Anyway, I met her on a plane to Vegas. Flew out there with a couple of guys to enjoy a weekend of blackjack. And what do you know? I almost married the little filly out there. You know Las Vegas is a marrying town. Anyway, just as I was about to say I do, I sobered up and caught the next plane back to Dallas. Whew, that was a close call.'' He took a hefty swallow of beer, then drained the glass.

"And when I read your ad, I told myself, Rex, this here gal's got the right idea. Approach a marriage in a businesslike way. Heck, I've tried every other way. Why not this one?''

"How many times have you been married?''

"Four. Five, if you count the two marriages to Adele.''

Lauren was a sensitive, polite person, and normally she would sit through any date, any dinner, any meeting—no matter how bored she was, no matter how miserable she was—but she knew she couldn't stand another minute of this luncheon with Rex Holley. "I'm sorry, Mr. Holley, but I don't think we're at all suited. You wouldn't be happy with me at all. So if you'll just excuse me...'' She picked up her handbag from the floor and headed toward the door, praying that he wouldn't follow her.

"Hey darlin', where ya going? What's wrong?'' She could hear his voice thundering behind her as she pushed open the front door. Everyone else could hear his voice, too. Lauren shuddered as she raced, head down, for her car. How embarrassing. Now she wouldn't be able to show her face again at one of her favorite restaurants. Lauren groaned as she hurried into her sports car and headed back toward her office.

"WELL?'' Casey was standing by the door as Lauren came in. "I'm waiting with bated breath for a report. How was Rex?''

"Not quite what I had in mind. We just weren't compatible,'' Lauren said, tight-lipped. The only woman who might be compatible with Rex Holley, she thought, was a woman who liked to eat a lot, listen a lot and was willing to give up thinking.

"Well, how about some details? As an active observer of this cockeyed scheme of yours, don't I deserve a blow-by-blow?"

"Don't ask. Please don't ask. It's depressing to think that Rex Holley is one of the hundred men that some hundred and fifty women, or whatever the ratio is, have to choose from." Lauren plopped into one of the chairs in the reception area. "I'm beginning to think you were right, Casey—maybe this was a stupid idea."

"Oh, you can't give up yet. Besides, there's still cocktails with George Farley." Casey tried to suppress a smile as she made reference to the third response Lauren had received.

"No way. In this instance, two strikes are definitely enough to call an out." She got up and went into her office, Casey trailing behind. "My head's killing me. I just want to go home and pull the covers over it." She reached into her purse for a small tin of aspirin and took two.

"Gee, that's too bad." Casey picked up a yellow telephone message on the desk. "Not only do you have another date, but while you were at lunch with Sexy Rexy, Bachelor Number One called."

"You mean George?"

"No, he's Bachelor Number Three. I mean your lawyer friend, Matt Kennerly." She handed Lauren the message. "Maybe he wants to make amends."

"He's probably calling about his fee—did I tell you he threatened to charge me?" She crumpled up the paper and tossed it into a wastebasket. "I don't care what he wants."

"I don't blame you. He sounded like a real jerk." The twinkle in Casey's eyes belied her words. She walked over to the wastebasket, retrieved the message and waved it in front of Lauren. "Mind if I return the call?"

Lauren grabbed the message. "I think you're kidding, but if there's anything I've learned today, it's not to take chances." She tore the message into tiny pieces and sprinkled them into the wastepaper basket.

Lauren's mind was definitely befuddled from the events of the day, but one thing was clear, she wasn't up to going out that night. Matthew Kennerly and Rex Holley were more than enough for one day. How much male mismatch could a girl take in twenty-four hours?

"So what are you going to do about George?"

"I'm going to call and cancel right now and then go home and go to bed." She fished on her desk for the phone number of Bachelor Number Three. He had written the number on his letter and she had called him earlier to make the date. Now she would call and beg off.

She dialed the number. "No answer. Now what do I do?"

Casey shrugged. "You could stand him up."

"Then I'd be just as rotten as Mr. Kennerly. No, I guess I'm stuck." Lauren sighed. "I hope those aspirin start working soon."

Lauren entered the bar at Laurel's a few hours later. She took a quick look around. Two couples at one table, three women at another, a mixed trio at the bar. The only lone male besides the bartender was sitting at a table for two in a corner. He glanced up, then rose and started heading Lauren's way. She breathed a sigh of relief. Although not as handsome as Matthew Kennerly, when compared with Rex Holley, the man looked sensational. He was dressed conservatively, in a dark suit, white shirt and striped tie. His shoes were shined and his hair neatly cut.

"Lauren?"

"George?"

"Right you are," he said, pointing the way to his table, where a half-filled glass sat waiting. "I went ahead and ordered a bourbon and water for myself. What would you like?"

"White wine, please." Well, so far so good, Lauren told herself. At least he didn't tell me what I should drink. Still, she was withholding judgment. After all, she had been impressed with Matt Kennerly for a few minutes, too.

"So tell me," she said, as the waitress set down a glass of wine, "what made you answer my ad?"

"You get right to the point, don't you? That's great. Actually I liked the no-nonsense way you cut through the dating ritual and went to the heart of the matter—a marital merger, so to speak. Such a sensible idea. As a matter of fact—" George reached into his pocket and pulled out a piece of yellow ruled paper "—I have taken the liberty of setting up a schedule for meeting that goal. I used the same concepts I use at work." He looked up from the paper and smiled. "I'm a corporate planner. Now this is how I see it."

For the next thirty minutes George described his operational planning system—O.P.S., he called it. And Casey considered *her* unromantic and mechanical, Lauren thought. This man was all business. He hadn't once glanced at the sensational view of downtown Dallas, or noticed the evening lights just starting to twinkle. All George was interested in was his calendar of events. He'd even planned the arrival dates of two children. Naturally there would be one boy and one girl—children wouldn't dare disturb George's master plan. And he'd added a dog, of course.

Lauren took a sip of wine. Never again, she told herself, never again. I should have listened to Casey. I should have listened to my own better instincts. She glanced at her watch. It was just about time to call it a day.

She finished off the wine and stood up. "Thanks for the drink, George. And for drawing up that plan." She pointed to the papers on the table. "It was very helpful. But actually, what it made me realize is that this isn't such a good idea. Some things in life have to happen naturally; I'm afraid a marital partner can't be selected like a piece of business equipment."

George's face was crestfallen as Lauren turned to walk away. She thought he was going to call her back, but he didn't. He was probably too astonished that his careful planning, all his work had gone for naught.

Lauren unlocked the door to her car and climbed inside. She inserted the key into the ignition, then leaned her head back against the headrest before starting the engine. She felt totally drained—almost woozy. She had only one glass of wine, but she could feel the effect of the alcohol. Then she remembered she'd had no lunch. There had been no breakfast that morning, either. She had been too nervous about her appointment with Matthew Kennerly. *Dummy,* she said to herself. *You know better than to drink on an empty stomach. Lucky, you're not too far from home.* Her head was now beginning to throb. A suitable ending to a truly miserable day.

CHAPTER TWO

THE PEAL OF THE TELEPHONE awakened Lauren with a start. Disoriented, she looked around the dark bedroom. She was fully dressed and curled up under the bedspread, too weary to change when she'd arrived home. She felt terrible. The ache in her temples had not been alleviated, and the continuous ring of the telephone only made her head hurt more. "Stop it," she begged the instrument, only to be ignored. The ringing continued. Finally Lauren's hand fumbled for the receiver. "Hello," she croaked.

"Now I understand why you were advertising for a companion. Anyone who's in bed alone at nine o'clock at night must be desperate. Or are you alone?"

Lauren didn't need to hear anymore. She recognized Matthew Kennerly's voice instantly. Damn him. She slammed the receiver down. Or tried to, missing the cradle and having to make several more attempts before the call was disconnected. No sooner had she turned over when the telephone rang again. This time she ignored the ring and got out of bed, escaping to the bathroom. Apparently he got the message, because the phone was silent for the rest of the night.

Lauren opened one eye and glanced warily at the bleeping digital clock on her bedside table. Six-thirty. She groaned and hit the snooze button. Another ten minutes passed before the bleep started again. She reached to turn it off, then flipped the covers off her body and lay there waiting for a surge of energy to propel her to her feet. No surge came.

Thank goodness the week was almost over, she mused, then sat up and eased her bare feet into the blue slides next to her bed. She sighed, as the escapades of the day before came to mind. Oh, well. Sometimes a girl had to kiss a lot of frogs before she discovered a prince. She rose and shuffled into the bathroom.

She entered the steamy shower and let the water cascade over her taut, slim body. It felt good, soothing enough to enable her to face the day ahead and forget the day before. She was ready to bounce back and let bygones be bygones. Almost. The only fly in the bygones ointment was Matthew Kennerly. For some reason putting him into the past was going to be difficult. Even now his voice still echoed in her ears and she could see vividly the dark eyebrows framing those gray granite eyes. Did he learn those intimidating stares in law school, or had he come by them naturally?

And why had he telephoned the night before? To continue his tirade, to get in the last word? Well, he hadn't succeeded. She had successfully cut him off. No matter how hard it might be, Lauren was going to make herself forget the irritating man and his sexy, mocking eyes, and stop her silly schoolgirl fretting.

She dressed quickly, grabbed a Granola Bar and a cup of instant coffee and headed outside. It was the kind of day Lauren loved—bright, crisp, the temperature pleasantly cool for a Dallas June. The morning sun was almost healing in its intensity. Lauren paused for a moment, savoring the smell of the honeysuckle by the fence, then remembered she was in a hurry and quickly got into her car.

A client was expected at the office in thirty minutes—it wouldn't do to be late. Business might be booming at Classic Interiors, but that didn't mean she and Casey could afford to offend clients. She backed out of the driveway and before long was on Northwest Highway.

Lauren unlocked the door and entered the office. She might as well straighten up and put on a pot of water. Casey was out on a call and Emily, their part-time secretary, had been down with a virus and wasn't expected in until after lunch.

She checked her appointment book. Two new clients to see today. The company was really growing, she thought proudly. Sometimes she wondered how the three of them managed—she and Casey and Emily. Maybe they should consider adding an assistant decorator. They could afford more help. And it looked as if they were going to need it.

The telephone rang and Lauren picked it up. "Classic Interiors," she answered.

"Don't hang up," a deep voice instructed. "This is Matt Kennerly."

As if he had to tell her. "Really, Mr. Kennerly—"

"Matt."

"Mr. Kennerly, we have nothing to talk about. I'm sorry about bothering you yesterday. It was all an embarrassing mistake. Now, would you please just leave me alone?"

"I can't do that. Actually I'm the one who should apologize. That's why I called. But you're not making it easy. Can't you give me a break and forgive me for being so rude yesterday?"

What was the man up to, Lauren wondered. She had the impression he didn't apologize to people very often, and despite the contrite voice on the other end of the line, she doubted he was sincere. After all, his courtroom training probably enabled him to sound any way he wanted. The thing to do was get rid of him. "Okay, you're forgiven. Now goodbye, Mr. Kennerly." She replaced the receiver in its cradle.

The telephone rang again. Good grief. Was it him again? Was he going to pester her all day? This was her business. She couldn't afford to let the phone ring unanswered as she had at home. "Classic Interiors," she said.

"Why didn't you tell me you were Lyle Grayson's daughter?" he asked.

"I really didn't feel my family background was relevant. Are you suggesting my proposal would have been more acceptable if I had mentioned who my father is?"

"No—I'm not saying that at all. It's just that I know Lyle. We put in some hours together on the United Way campaign. I never dreamed you were his daughter. It makes our meeting all the more interesting—although that's sort of hard to imagine. I found it pretty interesting as it was."

"Oh? That's certainly not the impression I got yesterday. But I really must go, Mr. Kennerly. I'm expecting a client."

"Don't go. I shouldn't have been such a cynic when you dropped in, but I guess when you're a divorce lawyer cynicism becomes the name of the game."

"Well, I'm afraid that's your problem. Goodbye." She started to move the phone away from her ear.

"Have dinner with me." His voice was soft. "I want to talk to you."

"No, thanks. I think you've said enough—can't you just leave well enough alone?"

"No. The only way I can adequately express my apologies is to buy your dinner. Okay?" His inquiry was met with silence. "Then how about an appointment," he said. "I was thinking about redecorating my office."

Lauren wanted to hang up again, but doubted it would accomplish anything. "Spare me," she muttered. She knew she shouldn't have gotten out of bed today. The day was going downhill quickly. "For the last time, goodbye, Mr. Kennerly." She heard him say "Matt" as she put the receiver down.

The door opened and Lauren's first client appeared. She was relieved that no more harassing phone calls came in while she was talking kitchens with Mrs. West. After looking at wallpaper books for a half hour she began to forget all about Matt Kennerly.

"Any calls?" Casey had just walked in, passing Mrs. West who was on her way out. She had a carton of juice in one hand and a small box of doughnuts in the other. "Ready for a coffee break?"

"Why not?" Lauren reached for a chocolate doughnut.

"Well, tell me all about George." Casey sat down in the arm chair beside Lauren's desk.

"You don't want to know. Believe me." Lauren took a bite of her doughnut.

"Not another Rex?" Casey asked, her eyes growing rounder.

Lauren shook her head. "No, not at all. George was genteel and actually didn't look half-bad. In fact, things were fine until he really started talking. After that it was unbearably boring. The man had designed a plan for the rest of our lives, including the two kids and the cocker spaniel."

"Wow." Casey reached into the sack for another doughnut. "Well, here comes five more pounds." She pinched a roll of fat around her waist and eyed Lauren. "Why is it you can eat like a horse and never gain an ounce?"

"Probably because I don't get much to eat at home. I'd starve without my jar of peanut butter and frozen dinners. I keep telling you there are a lot of advantages in not knowing how to cook."

Casey shrugged and looked through her appointment book on the counter. "Any calls?"

"Not any that I want to talk about."

"Uh-oh. Did one of your pen pals call again? Let me guess—Matt Kennerly."

Lauren nodded.

Casey's face lit up. Her large blue eyes began to sparkle. "Really? What did he want?" Her question was garbled by a mouthful of doughnut.

"To apologize. Or so he said."

"Terrific. Maybe your little scheme wasn't such a bad idea after all. By the way I, uh, found out a little something about your Mr. Kennerly last night." She took a sip of juice. "That guy's one great catch. You already told me he was gorgeous. Well, he's powerful and successful too—a divorce lawyer to the rich and famous."

"Too bad, 'cause I'm not interested. My strongest hope is that I never see his arrogant face again."

"I wouldn't bet the rent on that happening. He seems interested. And he sounds just like the sort of man you need."

"Are you serious? He's everything I don't need—or want. He's overbearing, egotistical, abrasive—"

"Sure, just what you need." Casey raised her hand to quiet Lauren's protest. "Maybe not what you think you want, Lauren, but what you need. Do you realize you're always going after the same kind of man you complain about? Bland, manageable? Mr. Vanilla? The kind of man your family's always fixed you up with. Then after a date or two, you're bored to death. I don't think Matt Kennerly would bore you.''

"He infuriates me. I wish he'd just leave me alone." She gestured with her coffee cup, some of the now cold liquid sloshing out in the process.

"Hey, he's really got you in a dither, hasn't he?" Casey took Lauren's mug and eyed the contents critically. "Let me make you a cup of tea—maybe that'll relax you." She plopped a tea bag into the rinsed cup and added hot water, dabbing the bag up and down.

"I think my headache's coming back," said Lauren, as she accepted the tea from Casey. "The tea will be good. Thanks."

"Tell you what I'm going to do—I'll screen the calls for the rest of the day. Will that help?"

Lauren smiled in spite of herself. "That'll be great." With Casey screening the calls, she wouldn't have to worry about talking to . . . people she didn't want to talk to. Lauren made an on-the-spot decision to ban a certain name from her vocabulary. She would carry on with the business of decorating and try to forget about dates and men and marriage mergers.

Right after lunch, Lauren left for a client's home in Lake Highlands, a beautiful residential area in the northeast part of the city. She was glad to get out of the office for a few hours, and the drive by White Rock Lake was just what the doctor ordered. The lake shimmered like silver in the sunlight and a few sailboats were skimming across the glittering surface. What she wouldn't have given to be out sailing herself.

On the return trip, cruising down Mockingbird Lane, Lauren eyed the lake wistfully again and, on impulse, pulled off the road and parked near a picnic table. She sat facing the lake and watched the wind play in the sails of the small craft.

What was she going to do with her life? Her grandiose plan to find a husband in the classifieds had definitely run aground. Now what? Acquiesce in her parents' matchmaking efforts again, consult a marriage broker, resign herself to spinsterhood? Lauren didn't know the answer.

All she knew was that she couldn't shed the restlessness she was feeling. It had come on about six months before, and continued to linger. Was it her last birthday that did it? Turning twenty-nine—the big Three-O looming ahead? Or was it something else? Whatever, it seemed to have affected her judgment. She shook her head ruefully and got up from the table. Oh well, maybe she could put the experience to good use. Perhaps she should write a book—*One Hundred and One Ways Not to Meet a Man*.

"CASEY, WHERE ARE YOU?" Lauren dumped her load of samples on the couch in the reception area.

"We're back here in your office," Emily called out. "Come see."

"Feeling better?" Lauren asked as she walked into her office. She didn't hear Emily's response. She was too astonished to listen. On her desk were four large vases, each filled with red roses—dozens of them. "Good Lord, what is this?"

"If I'm counting correctly," Casey answered, "it's a dozen dozen. And I just bet I know who sent them." She handed Lauren a card. "Come on, read it and tell me if I'm right."

Lauren had a premonition that she was. The card confirmed it. Why? she wondered. This little display must have set Matthew Kennerly back several hundred dollars. For someone who only the day before had criticized her for being a fortune hunter, he was sure throwing money her way.

"Well, what does it say?" Both Casey and Emily were waiting for her to read the card aloud.

Saved by the bell, thought Lauren, as the telephone rang. She rushed to answer, practically snatching the receiver out of Emily's hand. "Classic Interiors."

"Lauren?" It was Matt. Lauren mentally counted to ten. Why hadn't she let Emily take the call? Would she never learn?

"Did you get the flowers?" he asked. "Will you have dinner with me tonight?"

"Yes. No."

"I guess I can figure out which answer is which. So you got the flowers—hope you like roses."

"I do, but a hundred and forty-four is a bit excessive, don't you think?"

"I just wanted to show you how sorry I am."

"You've already apologized. And you've been forgiven."

"Prove it. Have dinner with me tonight."

"I can't have dinner with you tonight." Or ever, she thought.

"So you really don't accept my apology."

"I'm busy. I'm going to dinner at my parents' house."

"You could take me with you."

"Sorry. It's strictly a family affair."

"If you mean no, then just say so."

Lauren ran her fingers through her hair in a gesture of exasperation. "Would it do any good if I did?"

"Not really," he admitted. "I'm not used to taking no for an answer."

"Maybe you don't hear the word very often, Mr. Kennerly, and maybe you're not used to accepting it, but the answer is no. And that's that. There's no point in arguing about it."

"I agree. There's no point in arguing. See you later."

"What do you mean by that?" Lauren asked. But the only answer was a dial tone.

"Persistent, isn't he?" Casey was laughing again.

"Who's persistent?" Emily asked. "I think I missed something by being off sick this week. What's going on?"

"Disgruntled client," Lauren replied. "Could you please get rid of these things, Emily?" She gestured toward the vases of flowers. "Take them over to one of the hospitals, or something."

"Do we have to?" Emily sniffed one of the blooms. "They're so beautiful. It's hard to believe a disgruntled client sent them." She looked skeptically at Lauren.

"Don't ask any questions," Casey instructed Emily. "Just help me get them out to the car. It's too long a story to explain. And too unbelievable."

"And a closed book," Lauren snapped. "One I don't want opened ever again."

Casey winked at Emily as each of them grabbed a vase and walked out of the office toward the front door.

"PRINCESS. COME ON IN." Lyle Grayson kissed his daughter on the cheek as he greeted her at the door. "You're fifteen minutes late. I was afraid you weren't coming."

Lauren squeezed his arm. "You know me better than that. I just had some bills to take care of before I could leave the office. Since when does dinner with the Grayson family run on a tight schedule?"

"We'd be in trouble if it did—trying to get everyone together is not that easy." Lyle wrapped his arm around his daughter as they walked from the foyer toward the den. "Your brothers are out in the garden, and the girls are in the den with your mother. Oh, and I almost forgot, we have a special guest."

"A guest?" Lauren stopped suddenly. She knew it. But how? Just how had Matt Kennerly managed to finagle an invitation to her parents' house?

"Don't worry," her father whispered, "it's not what you think. Your mother hasn't found another suitor for you. You can relax." His voice returned to a normal level. "Come into the den and meet Dorothy."

A middle-aged woman was sitting on the couch with her mother, a photo album between them. "Oh, Dorothy, here's Lauren now." Lauren went over and shook the woman's hand. She gave her mother a quick hug and then greeted her two sisters-in-law, Dee and Melissa, who also were holding albums. "Lauren, this is Dorothy Davis, a wonderful neighbor from years past. Your father and I haven't seen her in ages. She and her husband moved away to Minneapolis when you were just a toddler. But she's on vacation here in Dallas, and while she was visiting with us, she wanted very much to see you children again."

"Oh, that's nice," Lauren said, relieved. Then she silently chided herself for being silly—running scared after an unfortunate encounter with someone she hardly knew and being afraid of running into him again. She looked at Dorothy. "I hope Mother's not overwhelming you with all those family photos."

"Well, we do have a lot of catching up to do," Dorothy said, "and the pictures bring back such nice memories." She pointed toward a photo. "Here's one of you with my son, Michael. The two of you learned to walk together. Now he's a high-school football coach."

Lauren was relaxing with a soda and lime, listening to Dorothy's reminiscences, when the doorbell rang. "That must be the messenger I was expecting," her father said as he placed his drink on the bar.

"Lyle, you promised." Jeanette Grayson turned to her guest. "All he ever does is work. Morning, noon and night."

"It's just someone delivering something I have to look at before I go into the office tomorrow, Jeanette. I promise I won't even open the envelope until breakfast."

"Well, I'm going to hold you to that. I don't plan to be a widow just because you've worked yourself to death. Now you girls are my witnesses. He promised no work tonight."

"Nag, nag," he said with a laugh, as he left the room and headed toward the front door.

Masculine voices could be heard from the foyer. "Matt, I didn't expect you to come by. Thought you were sending a courier."

"Well, since I was in the neighborhood, I decided to drop this off myself. I'm really pleased you're interested, Lyle. Could you give me a call in the morning?"

"Certainly. But don't rush off."

As soon as she recognized the voice in conversation with her father, Lauren knew her worst fears had materialized. Matt Kennerly had invaded her parents' home. And her privacy—again.

She gritted her teeth as she heard her father say, "Don't be ridiculous. Of course you're not imposing. Come on in and meet everyone."

Matt Kennerly walked into the den, flashing the same ingratiating smile he probably used for clients and jurors. He gave Lauren a quick glance before directing his attention to the two older women and acknowledging the introductions.

"Mrs. Grayson, I'm so happy to meet you at last— sorry to intrude on you like this," he said, not really looking sorry at all, Lauren thought.

But Jeanette Grayson cut him off before he could continue his apology. "Why, Mr. Kennerly, we're delighted you stopped by. And, of course, you'll join us for dinner."

He made a couple of feeble protests before allowing himself to be persuaded to stay for the meal. Lauren wanted to scream. He had managed to maneuver himself into their house, and now she would be forced to endure an entire meal with him.

"Mr. Kennerly, I want you to meet an old friend and neighbor," Jeanette said. Matt and Dorothy shook hands. "And this is Dee and Melissa, our daughters-in-law."

Matt greeted them. "Your husbands and I have played a little golf together."

Lauren could visualize tiny wheels beginning to turn in her mother's head as she realized she had both her daughter and a handsome eligible bachelor in her clutches in the same room.

Then Jeanette continued. "And this is our daughter, Lauren."

Matt turned to Lauren, giving her a quick wink that only she could see. "Hello, Lauren. You probably don't remember, but we've already met. I remember it vividly, of course. You were wearing a pink suit. Seems like it was just yesterday."

"Nice to see you again," she lied, offering her hand for a tense handshake.

Lyle Grayson came over and clasped Matt's shoulder. "Now, if you charming ladies will excuse us, Matt and I need to go quickly over a bit of business. I know I promised, Jeanette. But we'll only be a couple of minutes." He gestured Matt out of the room, and followed behind.

How convenient for Mr. Kennerly that he had important business to go over with her father tonight, Lauren thought. "I'm sure it was too urgent to wait until business hours tomorrow," she mumbled aloud.

"Did you say something, dear?"

"Sorry, Mother, I was just reminding myself of something I needed to do at work tomorrow."

Jeanette chuckled as she turned to the others. "Lauren is the only person I know who has conversations with herself—out loud."

The women chatted for a while, and at last Dorothy directed her full attention to Lauren and smiled. "So, your mother has told me how successful you are—and how busy. Tell me, do you have time for a man in your life?"

Lauren stifled a groan. Dorothy didn't know it, but she had just introduced her mother's favorite topic. How was she going to get out of a long, frustrating discussion about meeting Mr. Right?

"Well..." she began, but was saved from further comment by the reappearance of her father and Matt. In this instance, however, it was really only a trade of one unpleasantness for another.

Matt took the chair next to Lauren's. A sly grin crossed his face. "I believe you're a decorator, Lauren?"

"That's right," she answered stiffly, and then, in an effort to divert attention away from herself, added, "Actually my mother's a decorator, too—only she does it without pay. For friends and family. This room is a testimony to her talent." She gestured at the cardinal-red walls, the deep oak paneling, the oriental rug. Antiques were placed unobtrusively around the room and fresh flowers sat in an arrangement on a side table in front of a large Chippendale mirror. Part of the bookcase was given to family pictures, and an oil painting of the three Grayson children hung over the mantel of the brick fireplace.

"It's a lovely room, Jeanette," Dorothy agreed.

"Indeed," Matt said, turning back to Lauren. "If you have half your mother's eye for colors, you must be quite successful. Do you have to advertise much?"

Lauren choked on her drink. She began coughing and had to take several more sips before the coughing subsided and her beet-red face returned to its normal color. "Went down the wrong way," she explained.

Fortunately, everyone was distracted by the arrival of her brothers, Roger and L.J. "Matt," L.J. said, "what brings you here? It's been a long time since I've seen you at the club." Matt turned his attention away from Lauren and began talking with her brothers. The women returned to their picture albums and reminiscing until dinner was announced.

"Wonderful meal, Mrs. Grayson," Matt commented as they began eating. "You seem to be skilled in all the domestic arts." Jeanette had prepared coq au vin, wild rice and baby carrots, which were served by the maid, Rita.

"Being a homemaker is my career," she said proudly. "I keep telling Lauren that a happy home is the greatest gift a woman can have—with the right husband, of course. And Dee and Melissa agree with me."

Lauren shot warning daggers at her mother, but Jeanette averted her eyes and turned to Matt, asking him a question Lauren knew she already had the answer to. "Are you married, Mr. Kennerly?"

"No. And please call me Matt." He picked up a roll and started spreading it with butter. "I just haven't found the right woman. No time, I guess. But I'm not getting any younger. Maybe I need to take out a want ad." He laughed.

The group laughed, too, all except for Lauren who reached for the salt shaker and began salting her food vigorously, to avoid looking Matt's way. "I can't see how that would be necessary, Matt," Jeanette continued. "I bet the young women are beating a path to your door."

He laughed again. "Well, every once in a while one does appear in my office."

Lauren kept her eyes glued to her plate. She stabbed at a piece of chicken with her fork and brought it to her mouth. She was eating too rapidly; she always did when she was upset. If Matt Kennerly didn't get out of her life she'd gain ten pounds.

"And what kind of business deal are the two of you working up?" Jeanette asked Matt.

"Darlin', not now. You shouldn't ask that of a lawyer," admonished her husband.

"I don't mind, Lyle," Matt assured him. "I've got a little land in south Texas, Mrs. Grayson, and I've got an idea for developing it. I just wanted Lyle's opinion of the deal. No one knows business like a Grayson," he said, with a slight inflection on the word business.

Jeanette beamed, "Oh yes, I'm proud of my men," she said. If she only knew, thought Lauren, that the reference was not to the Grayson men, but a stab at her daughter. "Lauren's little business is also doing well," Jeanette said.

Lauren flinched. To her mother, her work would always be that "little business." Just a hobby until Mr. Wonderful came along. Well, her work was no hobby and Matt Kennerly was certainly not Mr. Wonderful.

"That's what I understand. I may hire her myself." He flashed a glance Lauren's way as he took another bite from his roll. "And when are the Grayson grandchildren due?" He cast his eyes at the obviously expectant Melissa and Dee.

Gad, thought Lauren, he's got Mother eating out of his hand and now he's working on my pregnant sisters-in-law. Those two like nothing better than talking about their babies.

"Only seven more weeks," Dee answered.

"At one point we hoped for the same day," Melissa chimed in. "But now I don't care as long as the baby is healthy and not late. I never realized nine months could be so long. I'm beginning to hate Lauren every time I look at her trim body."

"Lauren does have a nice figure," Matt agreed. "But you look beautiful just as you are, and I'll bet she secretly envies you and that little bundle of joy you're carrying."

Lauren reached for her glass of water, almost tipping it over. What was he trying to do, analyze her? If so, he was doing a darn good job. Admittedly she'd started having these feelings of unrest around the time she heard about the pregnancies. Maybe there *was* something to the maternal instinct, complicated by the fact that she wasn't getting any younger. She was already the same age as Dee and three years older than Melissa. Yes, she admitted, she was envious.

"I doubt that Lauren has her sights on motherhood," L.J. piped in. "She's going to be the ultimate career woman. She's too damn independent to get married."

"Besides," Roger taunted, "Lauren doesn't believe in love."

"Having two older brothers can turn you off men for life," Lauren shot back.

"Whatever happened to our adoring baby sister?" Roger directed his question to L.J.

"I don't know. But she's sure getting crotchety in her old age."

"Well, at least the rest of the male race has been spared her viper's tongue."

"Yeah, and her awful cooking, too. Do you remember the time—"

"Boys, enough." Jeanette scolded. "Will you two ever grow up? You tease her as much now as you did when you were teenagers. What will our guests think?"

Yes, Lauren mused. *We can't let this marriageable man think the wrong thing. Well, too late, Mother. He's already formed his opinion of your darling daughter.*

Jeanette got up and placed her napkin beside her plate. "I'll just check with Rita to see how the coffee's coming along. Why don't we have it in the living room?"

At her prompting, everyone got up and headed out of the dining room. Lyle escorted Dorothy, L.J. and Roger their respective wives, which left Lauren to trail along behind with Matt. "It looks like your mother has a beautiful flower garden." He gestured toward the French doors. "Care to get a breath of fresh air and show me the roses?"

"All right," she agreed. "Anything to get away from those two obnoxious siblings of mine." She glared at her brothers, then opened the doors to the patio.

"And," she added, as they moved out of earshot, "to give you a chance to explain how you maneuvered your way in here tonight."

"Can't," he said. "Professional secret."

She gave an exasperated sigh. "Well, the 'how' isn't really important anyway. But the result is. You've toyed with me in front of my family for nearly two hours."

"I'm sorry if I embarrassed you in there." Matt was holding her elbow as they walked down the sandstone path of the rose garden.

"Oh really? You seemed to be enjoying yourself quite a lot."

"Well, I was. But that's because you're so much fun to tease. Still, I am sorry."

"You apologize a lot, don't you?"

"I do, don't I? Just to you, though. Forgive me and have dinner with me tomorrow?"

"I'll forgive you. But I don't think dinner's such a good idea."

"Why not? I like your family. And you excite me. I suspect it'll never be boring when we're together. I'm ready to take you up on your ad and call the parson right now."

"You're still making fun of me."

"No. Not true. I've simply given the notion a lot of thought and decided the arrangement would be terrific. We'd be good together."

"You sure make up your mind quickly."

"If I'd had any sense I'd have pounced on the idea the minute I first saw you. If we get busy, you could be in the maternity ward not long after Dee and Melissa."

Lauren's cheeks blazed. "You're contemptible! Now that you've seen the roses, let's go back in."

"Not yet." He trailed a finger down her cheek. His head moved closer. Lauren glanced up with hesitation. His steely eyes bore into her, ensnaring her. Her heart was pounding against her ribs. He was going to kiss her. She felt his hand caress her neck, but then he moved away. "I'll pick you up about six tomorrow."

Lauren pulled back, feeling strangely disappointed. "I'm not going out with you. Can't you get that through your thick skull?"

"Well then, let's go back in. I've a very interesting story to tell Lyle and Jeanette."

"You wouldn't dare."

"Wouldn't I?" His challenging stare again reminded her that he was an attorney.

"Okay, I'll go out with you. Once. And I guarantee you'll have a miserable time." She flounced back into the house, leaving Matt standing alone in the garden. His laughter reverberated behind her in the summer night.

CHAPTER THREE

"BLACKMAIL—that's what it is, blackmail," Lauren muttered. She was talking to herself, pulling clothes from the closet, looking them over for a moment, then returning the hangers to the rods. Pandora, her gray Persian, sat on the bed, watching as if amused.

"He's the hotshot attorney. He knows blackmail is illegal, but he doesn't care. He's willing to use any means—fair or foul—to give me a rough time."

She pulled out a green silk dress. Perfect for revenge, she decided. Not only did the green accentuate her soft coloring, but the clingy material draped flatteringly over her breasts and hips. If she had to go on a date with Matt Kennerly, then she was going to wear the sexiest outfit in her closet.

Maybe he would fall hopelessly in love with her, and then she could spurn him for what she hoped would be the last time, tell him where to go!

"That's ridiculous," she said aloud. "Matt Kennerly's probably too cynical to ever fall in love. Especially when he spends every day as a killer shark, feeding off failing marriages."

Somehow the idea of all those marriages, people's dreams gone asunder, saddened her. One of the main reasons she'd placed her ad was to find a man who'd approach marriage in practical terms and keep passion out of the picture. Too bad the first encounter had to be with Matt. He seemed to have jinxed her whole campaign.

Then she was no longer sad, she was mad. Matt had already sparked one passion in her—anger.

Lauren gathered up the lingerie she'd laid out earlier and headed for the bathroom.

She poured a dollop of bath oil into the circular tub, then ran the water, the spray turning the yellow liquid into fine bubbles. She untied the sash of her black-flowered kimono and let it drop to the floor. Tentatively she stuck a toe into the water to test the temperature. It was just right, and she stepped in. Maybe a long soak would relax her taut nerves. She'd need all her wits about her to deal with Matt.

He'd kept her on edge for the past three days. First the meeting in his office, then the roses, then the farce at her parents' house, and today throwing the whole courting ritual at her—two phone calls and a bouquet of mixed blossoms sent to her office. She wouldn't be surprised to see him show up with a heart-shaped box of candy under his arm. But one question plagued her. Why was he bothering with all this? He'd done a one-hundred-and-eighty-degree turn since their first meeting in his office. Despite his comments at her parents' house about re-thinking her proposition, Lauren couldn't help but be suspicious.

To Matt this was probably all a great big joke—at her expense. Maybe he'd had such a good time teasing her the night before that he was coming back for more. Or else he was taking his fee out in a pound of flesh—her flesh.

Well, whatever he was up to, there was no backing out now. Matt said he would be there promptly at six and it was already five-thirty. The plan was to have a quick drink somewhere, then go on to the Fair Park to see *The Music Man*.

It would normally be Lauren's favorite kind of evening—going to the theater, and especially to the Music Hall. She remembered her childhood visits there. After the performances her mother would take her to the stage door to get a closer look at some of the stars. Those had been fairy-tale evenings. But tonight would be no fantasy. More likely a bad dream—one, unfortunately, she would have to live with. No waking up and finding that none of it had happened.

SHE HEARD A CAR DOOR SLAM. Six o'clock. He was right on time. Drat the man. He was proving to be a major annoyance.

Lauren let the bell ring twice before she answered. "I thought maybe I'd been stood up," Matt drawled when she finally opened the door.

"Now, I wouldn't have dared do that, would I?" Lauren answered challengingly. "Then I'd have you announcing to the world my desperate attempt to find a husband."

He was standing with one arm propped against the doorway, obviously relaxed. There wasn't a hint that he was experiencing anything similar to the turmoil rumbling within Lauren, which irritated her even more.

"Afraid I'd put a notice on the front page of the *Morning News*?" he teased.

"Is that the kind of evening this is going to be?" she snapped.

"I hope not, Lauren." His voice was gentle, calm. He traced a finger down her cheek. "Aren't you going to invite me in?"

She moved aside to allow him entrance, not at all sure that she wanted him to come in—that she wanted to share her private space with him. Matt seemed to be taking over, and worse, she seemed at a loss as to how to stop him. She felt she was losing control.

There was something about his touch, even the gentle stroke of his fingertips, that intrigued her and made her long for more. She shouldn't feel this way, she told herself. It might be different if Matt were serious about her; then perhaps she could indulge her desire for his touch.

But he wasn't serious. And even if he were, was he what she needed? He had said at their first meeting that he didn't want a wife, but what if he'd been in earnest when he said he'd changed his mind? That he was ready to call the parson?

Successful men generally didn't want to play second fiddle to a woman's career. Not that she intended to put her career ahead of everything, but her business was important to her. Besides, she'd be a total flop in a house-wife role. She had neither the skills nor the inclination to be a full-time wife.

"Nice place," he said. "It's obvious an interior decorator lives here." His eyes took in the living room and the second-story landing visible in the high-ceilinged entry. He walked into the kitchen. "Spacious, too." Pandora rubbed against his leg. "Pretty cat." He scratched her head.

"I'm glad you approve." Lauren reached for her purse on the kitchen counter. "Well, I guess we'd better go."

"We've still got time," he said, continuing to look around. His perusal irritated Lauren. She didn't like the way he was studying her place—or her. He was giving her the same kind of survey she'd received in his office. "Green is my favorite color," he said, "but I never realized how good it could look on a woman." A sly smile crossed his lips. "Maybe we'd better leave, after all."

"This will never get off the ground if you don't relax a little." Matt and Lauren were sitting at a table on the patio of Dakota's, the splash of the waterfall obliterating the street sounds of downtown Dallas.

"I am relaxed," Lauren fibbed. She doubted she could ever be truly relaxed around Matt. The man exuded sexual charisma. That was precisely it, she thought. Sexual charisma. Somehow the thought made her feel better, as if she'd stumbled onto Matt's secret—the reason she'd always felt at a disadvantage in his company. She was reacting to his charisma, just like the majority of his female clients probably did. He was a hard man to be indifferent to.

"We've got about an hour," he said glancing at his watch. "Would you like something to eat, or just a drink?"

Lauren smiled. The first real smile she'd given Matt. His question had brought back thoughts of Rex Holley.

"Are you going to share the reason for that smile?" he probed. "Or is it a private joke?" Suddenly his hand moved to take hers. "You're very beautiful, Lauren."

Lauren sat mesmerized for a moment, then pulled her hand away. "I don't think so." Her teasing answer belied the electrifying sensation his touch created.

"Oh, I don't just think, I know you're beautiful," Matt responded. "And I'm sure you've looked into the mirror lately."

"I didn't mean that. I meant I'm not going to tell you why I was smiling."

"Then you agree you're beautiful?"

"Do you ever leave the courtroom, Mr. Kennerly?"

"I'll leave the courtroom anytime for you. Just say the word."

"Daiquiri."

"You're a master at changing the subject, Ms Grayson."

"Changing the subject? Didn't you ask me if I'd like a drink?"

"Touché. But of course." He signaled for the waiter.

"I love this restaurant," she said. "Do you come here often?"

"As often as I can. It's one of my favorites. An outdoor oasis below street level. Reminds me a little bit of New Orleans."

Their drinks before them, Lauren decided it was time to get down to business. She smiled again. Business. She had a suspicion Matt could make her totally forget not only business but everything else. Maybe even the day of the week. "Why were you so insistent I go out with you?"

"A lot of reasons. For one thing, I felt rotten about what happened in my office. Obviously someone was playing a joke—on both of us. I usually have a better sense of humor, but it deserted me that day."

He took a sip of his drink. "I'd been in court for two days. A really messy case. Mud slinging, threats. I'm convinced my client's the wronged party. I've seen the black eyes and the bruises.

"The husband's got a lot of witnesses and is making all sorts of claims." He held his glass in the air. "Says she's an alcoholic, on drugs, an unfit mother—you name it. I'm not sure how it's going to turn out. The guy's got good legal help. But I'd sure like to see him get what's coming to him—and I'd like to be the one to do it."

"You really do care, don't you?"

"Is that so surprising?" Matt shrugged. "Well, enough shop talk. I only mentioned the case to explain why I wasn't at my best the day you came in. Could you maybe give me another chance?"

Lauren wasn't sure what she should say. He did sound sincere, and he even looked a little contrite.

"Good," he said, accepting her silence as assent. "And now I have a question for you." He frowned. "Why does a woman like you—young, wealthy and, yes, beautiful, have to put an ad in the newspaper to find a man? Surely you only have to crook your finger to have a man drop everything and come running."

Lauren gave an exaggerated sigh. "It's not that simple. I've met men, lots of them. I can't tell you how many times my family or friends have fixed me up with dates."

"So what's the problem? If it's that you're too particular, I don't think you'll find the answer in the want ads."

"Maybe I am too particular. At least that's what a lot of people tell me. But I don't think so. It's just that I haven't found anyone I could imagine living with for the rest of my life—or anyone willing to accept me the way I am." That was partially true, Lauren thought.

"Prince Charming hasn't come riding up on his white charger, to carry you away and take care of you, hmm?"

"I didn't expect you to understand." She picked up the straw from her drink and began twisting it in her fingers. "I'm not looking for some prince to take care of me. I can take care of myself."

"Can you?" His look said he didn't believe her.

"This is not getting us anywhere," Lauren replied. "Why don't we just skip the musical and call it a night. I don't see the need to waste any more of our time."

Matt picked up her hand and cradled it in his. "And have you go away mad? Never. Look, maybe your notion of a marital merger isn't so bad after all. You just may be on to something. After all the divorces I've seen, I know I'd prefer an eyes-open approach to marriage."

Lauren smiled. His touch was calming. "That's what I told myself when I was dreaming up that little ad. That and the fact that I've been getting a lot of pressure from my family. Twenty-nine and single is unheard of in the Grayson family. Even though my brothers tease me and call me a confirmed, hopeless old maid, they'd still like to see me married. I'm supposed to be settled down and pregnant like my sisters-in-law. You saw how they all were—I'm getting downright paranoid about even going over there. Even Melissa and Dee have got into the act."

Now it was Matt who was smiling. "I get that treatment myself sometimes. Not from my folks—they're no longer living, and they were divorced, anyway. But my friends are always telling me that I've become too jaded and set in my ways. And they're probably right," he admitted. "Anyway, I thought maybe if we dated a little, we could find out if we're compatible. Then who knows? Maybe we'll carry through with the rest of your plan. Are you willing to give it a try?"

"I'm not sure." Her calm voice camouflaged the excitement his question raised. Lauren couldn't understand why she felt that way. She wasn't sure she even liked the man, and she still doubted his sincerity.

"Well, think about it." Matt drained his glass. "Want another fast drink? We need to leave in a few minutes."

Lauren looked down at the near-empty glass in front of her. "No, I'm fine. You go ahead if you like."

He shook his head and gestured for the check. When the waiter placed it on the table, Matt pulled a bill from his wallet. "Ready to go?"

Lauren had difficulty keeping her mind on the performance that evening. *The Music Man* had always been special to her. She had played Marian the Librarian in her high-school production and had spent many an evening since singing the music. Her favorite tune was "Good Night, My Someone." But tonight her mind was wandering. Could Matt possibly be her someone?

The evening had undergone a subtle change. Matt was no longer teasing, goading. Instead he was charming. And Lauren couldn't help responding. It was so pleasant sitting there beside him, his hand holding hers. During intermission they'd run into a couple of female acquaintances of Lauren's, and she'd felt a wave of satisfaction from the way they looked at Matt, the envious glances they sent her way. As the musical drew to an end, and Marian and Professor Hill were singing "Till There Was You," Lauren wondered what kind of spell Matt was weaving around her.

"HUNGRY?" Matt asked as they walked toward his car, a Mercedes coupe. "I haven't had a bite since lunch."

"Me neither," Lauren admitted. "But I don't usually eat this late."

"Why don't we stop at Kip's? They serve breakfast at all hours. We could get a head start on tomorrow." He opened the car door for Lauren and she slipped inside.

As they rode through the neon panorama of night-time Dallas Lauren glanced at the handsome man at the wheel. Matthew Kennerly was charming and entertaining—when he put his mind to it—and he'd definitely been putting his mind to it that evening. But were they right for each other?

Matt was obviously accustomed to running the show, to taking charge, no doubt even bullying people who stood in his path. He would probably expect a woman to be the good little wife, like Melissa and Dee. Domesticated like Lauren's mother. Maybe giving up a career and staying home.

That wasn't for Lauren. She wanted a partnership, not to be bossed around by some male. If she was going to seriously consider going through with her plan it was necessary to clear the air—the sooner the better.

Matt pulled the car into a parking space in front of Kip's Restaurant. They went inside and were ushered to a booth by the window. The waitress came quickly and took their orders for omelets and coffee.

Lauren picked at her paper napkin. "Before we go any further, I probably ought to make sure we're communicating."

"About what?"

"I don't want you to think back to the Grayson family dinner and get the wrong impression about me."

"I'm not following." He looked confused.

"You saw the kind of relationship my folks have. Hard-working father, domesticated stay-at-home mother. My brothers' marriages are the same way. And that's fine for them. But it's not what I want. I want just what I said in the ad—a partnership. Of equals. I'm not domestic and I don't want to be. I don't cook. I don't clean. And I don't do windows."

Matt began laughing, leaning his head back in loud guffaws.

"I'm not kidding," Lauren went on. "Men want someone to fuss over them, to wait on them, to be there when they come home. I just can't have my business and be the 'little woman' at the same time.''

"Believe it or not, I understand. I've met women who think they'd like to be a lawyer's wife, but when they discover how many hours I have to work, how many nights I put in, then the picture changes.''

"Exactly.''

"So what made you think that's what I want?''

Lauren gave a noncommittal shrug. "I just assumed that's what most men want.''

"But I'm not most men. Don't ever forget that.'' He smiled.

It was after midnight when Matt and Lauren headed back to her place. The evening had been fun—the last part especially. Lauren couldn't remember a more pleasant one in a long time. She'd enjoyed the honest conversation.

Clearly Matt was more than just a handsome face, and he seemed to be somewhat understanding. But was he serious about pursuing her plan? That was the question plaguing her. And if he was serious, could she trust herself to keep to the plan? Would she ruin it herself? Relationships with men sometimes made women do foolish things.

They could hear chirping of cicadas when Matt turned off the car's engine. "It's been a nice evening,'' she said. "Thank you.''

She started to open the car door, only to have Matt reach across and stop her. "I'll walk you to the door.''

"That isn't necessary.''

"I still believe in old-fashioned courtesy. What's the matter, Lauren? Frightened?''

Lauren opened her mouth in protest, then closed it. What was the use? If she argued, it would only confirm that she was indeed nervous about his seeing her to the door. She shrugged and waited while he climbed out of the car and came around to open her door. They strolled up the walk to the front door.

Lauren pulled a key from her handbag and inserted it into the lock. She stepped down into the foyer and punched a code to deactivate the security alarm, then turned to Matt. "Good night. Thanks again."

He remained on the top step, towering above her like a parent over a child. His look was in no way parental, though. He came inside, pushing the door closed with his foot and moving his head toward hers.

Lauren had wondered how that sensuous mouth would feel on hers. She was frightened, yet the fear faded as his lips, soft and tender, touched hers like a gentle puff of air, then moved away. She wanted more. More of the tingling sensation his brief kiss had evoked.

Her longing was not in vain. In moments Matt's mouth was on hers again, still gentle, but surer. No longer tentative, his kiss showed the expertise she knew he would have. For seconds they stood there, exploring the senses. Matt's hands were at her waist, not pulling her closer nor pushing her away. Simply holding her.

Lauren moved nearer, easing her arms around Matt's neck, weaving her fingers into the soft, thick hair at the back of his head. Her body was like a newly kindled fire, ready to burst into full flame.

As though sensing her compliance, Matt pulled her closer. His hand slid from her waist to the swell of her hips. Lauren made no protest. She wanted his lips on hers, his body tight against hers. Lauren was lost to everything but her feelings. Only when Matt's hand moved to her breast did she awaken from the spell he had cast over her. Her arms dropped from his shoulders, and she pressed her hands against him, pushing him away.

"Frightened, Lauren?" he asked again, a twinkle in his eyes giving evidence of his amusement. He looked as though he were thoroughly pleased with his performance—and hers.

His question annoyed her. It brought back her earlier concern that he might be toying with her. "Not frightened. Merely cautious. That's enough of an experiment for one night, don't you think?"

"Is that what it was—an experiment? All part of your plan?" His voice sounded calm, but there was a hint of anger in his eyes.

"What else?" she asked.

"Well, if we're experimenting, then we should take this audition to its full course, don't you think?" His hand moved to the top button of her dress. She stood spellbound as he deftly undid the silk-covered fastening. His hand moved to the second button.

"What do you think you're doing?"

"Experimenting. Just experimenting." The second button loosened. He ran a finger down the throbbing vein of her neck. "You react well to experimentation, Lauren. I think I'm going to enjoy this." He bent to place another gentle kiss on her lips, then turned and opened the door. Before Lauren realized what was happening, he was gone.

IT WAS THREE in the morning, and Lauren hadn't had a moment of sleep. She felt as though her life had turned topsy-turvy and that there was no way she could get it back on an even plane. Her body was still heated with desire. She couldn't deny that. But why, why did everything have to be turning out this way?

She didn't want to fall in love—she certainly hadn't banked on it. "Silly girl," she spoke aloud in the darkness, "this isn't love. This is plain old lust. The man turns you on." Still, love or lust, she wanted neither one until she saw the lay of the land.

She had the fleeting feeling she would be in danger with Matt Kennerly. He was too compelling, too sexy. His effect on her seemed to be beyond her control.

She pounded the pillow, trying to get comfortable. Nothing was out of her control, she told herself. All she had to do was play it cool. Not appear overanxious and not let him get the upper hand.

"DINNER?" It was only nine o'clock and already Matt was calling the office.

Lauren knew she should say no. She didn't want to appear too eager. Sure she'd placed the ad, but still, she didn't want Matt to get the wrong idea. Then any inclination to refuse his invitation flew out the window. She wanted to see Matt again. And she wanted to see him that evening. "What did you have in mind?" she answered, her voice a soft purr.

"That's a dangerous question," Matt said with a laugh. "What I was thinking about before I called was something a little more intimate, more romantic, than Kip's. Do you like The Grape?"

"Yes, very much." Lauren's voice was low, throaty. She'd have thought it an affectation in anyone else, but now the breathless sound came quite naturally.

"I'll pick you up at seven-thirty then. Bye for now."

Lauren was still sitting with the telephone receiver in her hand when Casey walked in. Her friend took the receiver and replaced it in the cradle. "No need in my asking how the date went last night. Maybe I need to rethink placing an advertisement.''

Lauren smiled. "Maybe you should.''

The rest of the day dragged, perhaps because of Lauren's anticipation of the coming evening. And when it came, Lauren couldn't have written a more perfect scenario. There was a wisp of a breeze in the summer air, the moon was a full, golden orb, and Matt was witty, entertaining, romantic. They lingered at the restaurant over wine, then coffee, and lots of conversation. She learned he gave his aunt the mumps when he was ten, and she told him about the time her brothers helped her climb a tree, then refused to assist her in getting down. She'd had to sit in the tree two hours waiting for her mother to come home. They left the restaurant after eleven and drove home the scenic way, along the meandering Turtle Creek.

Lauren was ready for Matt's good-night kiss when they got to her place. She gave no resistance as his hand stopped hers from reaching to turn on the light; instead he took her hand and placed it on his shoulder, his head bent toward hers. Lips touched lips, the kiss deepened, and again Lauren's body reacted to the closeness of Matt's as her other hand moved around his neck. But tonight he didn't linger. Teasing words didn't come. Instead he stepped away from her. "I'll call you.'' Then he was gone.

THE FOLLOWING WEEK Lauren jumped every time the telephone rang. *I'll call you...I'll call you.* Matt's words played over in her head a thousand times. She had believed him and had thought they were at the beginning of something special. Well, he'd certainly cleared up that misconception. She felt truly miserable. So much for playing it cool.

Then finally he did call. "How about dinner tonight?"

"Sorry. I don't think so."

"You're mad, aren't you? You've been feeling neglected." His voice had a satisfied ring to it. Something that told Lauren he knew she'd been waiting for his call.

"Of course I'm not mad. I'm just busy, that's all. I have a meeting this afternoon and I'm not sure how late I'll be."

"Tomorrow then?"

"I'm busy tomorrow, also."

"When are you free?"

"How about a year from next Wednesday?"

Matt chuckled. "I'm a patient man. But not that patient. Could it be that you're afraid?"

"Drop the challenges, Matt."

"Admit it. You are afraid. There was a spontaneous combustion between us. You can't deny that."

"I'm not trying to deny anything. And I'm not afraid. We'll just have to make it another time."

"Aren't you worried I might follow up on my threat to tell all?"

"Tell anyone you please, Matt. Give the evening news an interview. I simply don't care. It won't be the first time in my life I've lived through a little embarrassment. If it gets too bad, I can always leave town."

His deep laugh sounded over the line. "I couldn't be the cause of that. Dallas—and I—would never recover from losing you. Now please, have dinner with me. What do you say?"

"I still say no."

"Lauren, I know I should have called sooner. But I was working like a mule all last week, weekend included. Haven't had a minute to myself. But that's not all. I'll be honest with you. I wanted us to have a little time apart. A test, if you will, and it told me a lot. I don't know how you've felt the past week, but I know what it's been like for me. I've missed you. I want to see you, Lauren. Tonight."

His speech broke down all Lauren's resistance. She wanted to see him, too. And he sounded serious. As if he'd really missed her. Should she take a chance? She wasn't sure. "But I really do have to work late."

"I'll bring dinner in then. Maybe rent a movie to watch on the VCR."

Lauren only had time to change out of her work clothes into a red jogging outfit when she heard Matt at the door. Apparently he had come straight from his office, because he was dressed in a suit. He leaned over to give her a quick kiss, then shoved a pizza box into her hand. "I hope you like mushrooms and pepperoni."

He followed Lauren inside. She watched him as he set a brown paper bag on top of the television and pulled out several video tapes. "Take your pick," he said. "*The Sound of Music, Gone with the Wind* or *The Texas Chainsaw Massacre.*"

"You're kidding."

"Just testing to see if you were paying attention. Actually the last one is *Casablanca.*"

"Oh, I love that one. I've seen it at least eight times."

"Oops."

"No, I'd love to see it again."

"Great." Matt reached into the bag again and pulled out a bottle of Chianti. "I think pepperoni pizza calls for red wine, don't you?"

"Definitely," she said.

Lauren went into the kitchen and was about to reach into a cabinet for a couple of dinner plates when Matt came hurrying over. "Oh no. I'm not here to be waited on. You go sit down. I'll attend to everything." He took off his jacket and hung it over a kitchen chair, then loosened his tie and rolled up his shirt sleeves. "Now I'm ready to work."

Matt led her over to the kitchen table and pulled out a chair. "You just park yourself there and tell me where everything is."

With Lauren's assistance, he found the forks and napkins. He opened the refrigerator. "I see you don't eat in a lot." He stared at the nearly bare shelves, the only contents a bottle of Perrier, a carton of orange juice, a jar of peanut butter, a half-eaten frozen dinner and a large package of M&M's.

"Not too much. Most of my food comes from take-out counters or the store freezer."

Matt opened the freezer compartment. It was stuffed with more of the dinners. "I see what you mean. If we ever have a brownout, you'll starve to death."

He fished around for a corkscrew, poured two glasses of wine and handed one to Lauren. "To prepared foods and the classifieds," he said.

"Just when you were beginning to sound like a nice guy," Lauren answered, pausing with her wineglass in midair, instead of bringing it to her mouth for the toast.

"I am a nice guy. I can do better. How about, 'Here's looking at you, kid.'" He winked.

They propped themselves in front of the television, each with a glass of wine in one hand and a slice of pizza in the other. About two hours later, when the picture came to an end, Lauren was dabbing at her eyes with a napkin as Humphrey Bogart walked off into the fog.

Matt took the napkin from her hand and patted away a tear. "The Bogart character's a fool," he said. "I would never let the woman I love fly off on a plane and out of my life." He reached for the wine bottle on the coffee table and filled their glasses, then set the empty bottle on the floor.

"Oh, and what would you have done in Bogart's place?"

"How about this?" Matt leaned over and kissed her.

She leaned her head back against the sofa cushion and smiled as she looked at Matt. His eyes, which at their first meeting had been as hard as granite, were now a soft, fluid, almost mercurial gray. Matt set his glass down and put his arm around her shoulder, pulling her body closer to his.

Again he pressed his lips against hers, but this time they lingered as he enveloped her in the circle of his embrace. As if she were no heavier than a rag doll, he pulled her into his lap, cradling her head against his shoulder.

Lauren closed her eyes and felt Matt's lips gently brush each lid. The subtle smell of his after-shave filled her nostrils, and his warm breath tickled her cheek. She felt so comfortable in his arms; she wanted to stay there forever. She put her head against his chest and listened to the rapid thump of his heart. It sounded as though Matt had no more control over his body than Lauren had over hers when she was with him.

Instantly his lips claimed hers again, forcing her mouth to open slightly. The quick touch of his tongue sent a jolt of excitement coursing through her veins. His hands were strong against her back and the crush of his chest almost drew the breath from her.

Matt pulled his lips from hers and moved his mouth to her neck. She caressed his soft hair, as his lips moved down her throat. He pulled on the zipper of her jogging top. "No," she whispered gently.

"Why not?" he whispered back, his voice muffled by the material.

"Because." Lauren slowly pushed his head away and eased out of his lap. "I'm not ready."

"Oh, but I think you are. As ready as I am."

Lauren didn't respond. Matt was right—she was ready. In all her years, she'd never been more ready. He had pushed all the right buttons, and all the feelings she'd never felt, the feelings she'd assumed were Hollywood make-believe, were now coming to the surface. It was probably only a matter of seconds before she'd agree to anything....

"Marry me, Lauren."

"What? You're crazy."

"All I'm doing is answering your ad. You wanted a husband—here I am. Were you serious, or do I have to sue for false advertising?" His voice was a low rumble, his breathing still heavy.

"You once told me you didn't want to get married."

"And I once told you I'd reconsidered."

"I thought you were joking."

"Well it doesn't matter now, does it? I've definitely changed my mind."

"I think all the heavy breathing is getting to you," Lauren said. "Anyway, we can't get married. What would everyone say?" Her argument sounded hollow to her own ears. For the first time she realized the seriousness of her plan, and it frightened her. Was she actually considering it—considering marrying a man she barely knew? Someone who severely disturbed her equilibrium? Someone she feared caring about, perhaps because she knew she might start to care too much?

"Are you kidding? They'd say 'About time—we've been trying to get her married off for twenty-nine years.'"

"No, I mean, it's so soon. We met less than two weeks ago. We hardly know each other."

Lauren knew her comments made no sense to Matt. She felt like a blathering fool, seeking a stranger for a husband and then balking because she didn't know him well enough. But somehow she was beginning to prefer her idea in theory rather than practice.

"Is it references you want? I could probably get a judge or two to vouch for me. Or you could call my old Boy Scout leader. He would tell you how reverent, thrifty and brave I was as an Eagle Scout."

"Don't be ridiculous. It's more than that. For one thing, what's in this for you? Why are you being so persistent?"

"There are plenty of reasons. Monogamy is making a comeback these days. Perhaps I want to be on the cutting edge of this new trend."

"This is serious, Matt." She frowned.

"I am serious. I think we'd be good together. I'm ready to settle down, too. We know there's chemistry between us."

"Chemistry's not enough."

"It's half the battle. We'll worry about the rest later."

"Later may be too late," she protested.

"Are you looking for guarantees? Marriage doesn't come with a warranty, I'm afraid—and I should know." He pressed a brief kiss on her lips. "Where's the adventurous lady who placed that newspaper ad?"

"Long gone. Replaced by the other Lauren—the cautious Lauren. There are so many details, so many things to think about."

"Forget all the details. We'll pick up a license tomorrow and have a simple little wedding later in the week. Then we can honeymoon at my ranch—no reservations needed, no hassles."

"Are you sure you want to do this?"

"Positive." His voice was firm, certain.

Lauren believed him. He wanted to marry her. She still wasn't clear why. Maybe he was being honest, maybe he really did want to settle down, have a home and family. Women don't have a monopoly on those kind of feelings. "I don't know what to say."

"Say yes."

"This is crazy."

"Say yes, Lauren. It's such a little word."

"Yes."

CHAPTER FOUR

LAUREN PULLED HER CAR into the parking lot across from the County Records Building. She opened the door, then sat for a moment, staring nervously at the landmarks around her. The red Victorian courthouse, the Kennedy Memorial, John Neely Bryan's log cabin. Maybe she shouldn't have come. In the light of day her decision to marry Matt was beginning to seem even more impulsive, more foolish. A glance at the gloomy old Records Building where she was headed only served to reinforce her negative thoughts. Lauren reluctantly got out of her car. A soft breeze played with the skirt of her black-and-white floral dress as she waited for the light to change.

Diffidently she entered the building and took a seat on one of the worn wooden benches in the lobby. Matt was in court across the street and had picked this location as the most convenient spot for them to meet. She sat primly, hands folded across her purse, watching the people as she waited. Most seemed preoccupied—none were smiling, some looked downright grumpy. But then, why wouldn't they be? For the most part, this was a place to pay taxes or buy license plates or settle estates. Lauren began to feel she fit right in. Her anxiety level was rising fast.

She glanced at her watch. Fifteen minutes had gone by. She checked the clock across the hall to be sure it had the same time. Yes, eleven-fifteen. A young couple holding hands passed in front of her—the first people she'd seen smiling. It was obvious they were headed for the marriage-license bureau. Lauren could tell just by the matching expressions they wore—contented, self-satisfied, euphoric. She felt a twinge of jealousy. That was the way it was supposed to be—not the stomach-churning, close-to-nausea feelings she was experiencing.

Why had she let Matt talk her into this? Another glance at her watch—he was now thirty-five minutes late. Without him here to beat down her reservations, their agreement to be married seemed more and more ridiculous. But she couldn't back out now. Matt wasn't going to let her.

The night before he had asked if she'd been serious about wanting a husband, and she'd had to admit she was. A home and children were still on her agenda—but was this the best way to go about achieving her goals, and at such lightning speed? After all, if a business marriage was a viable idea—and that was a big if—what harm would it do to take a little more time to think it over, to be sure? Why was Matt in such a hurry? He might not have qualms, but she did. She needed more time—at least a few more weeks, or months, to be sure this relationship was right. When Matt arrived, that's exactly what she would tell him, she decided.

But what if he wasn't coming? For the first time, Lauren entertained the notion that Matt might have stood her up. Could this be the ultimate humiliation, his final retaliation for being subjected to her stupid advertising scheme? Her neck felt hot at the possibility she had been played for a fool, taken in by a glib, fast-talking attorney. She considered heading for the exit, then thought better of it.

Admittedly she didn't know Matt very well, but Lauren refused to believe he'd go that far just for revenge. During their conversation the night before—aside from the lapses into sarcasm—he had seemed completely frank. It was possible, and getting more probable with each passing minute, that after putting a little distance between hot desire and cold reality—he had simply reached the same conclusion she had. That marriage to a near-stranger wasn't something to rush into.

But she thought he'd at least have the decency to call instead of letting her drag down there and cool her heels for an hour. So what was she to do now—keep waiting or bolt for the door? *I'll give him one hour,* she decided. *If he isn't here by then, I won't be, either.* It was eleven forty-five. She would wait another fifteen minutes. Not one minute more.

She concentrated on the traffic in the hallway once again. Eleven-fifty. A group of tourists appeared and asked her for directions to the Reunion Arena. She rose from the bench, pointed and explained, then sat back down as the group departed.

Eleven fifty-five, fifty-six. "Okay, Lauren, you naive fool," she muttered under her breath, "you've wasted enough time." As she rose from the bench, she saw Matt rushing down the hall.

"Glad you're still here," he said. He was out of breath. "I was afraid you might think you'd been jilted."

His attempt at playfulness did not sit well with Lauren. "What happened?" she groused, making no effort to hide her disgruntled feelings.

"The session ran longer than I thought. We were in the judge's chambers and there was just no way I could leave." He slipped an arm around Lauren's waist. "That's going to be one of the nice things about our kind of marriage—having a wife who doesn't get all mad and pouty because my work comes first.''

Mad and pouty was exactly how she felt, and he knew it. She hated to be kept waiting. But she said nothing. After all, Matt was right. They had spent a lot of time talking about the importance of their careers. It was time to put her money where her mouth was, so to speak. She had arrived at the crossroads—her personal D day, D for Decision. She could walk out on this arrangement right now, or she could go along with the scheme, the scheme, after all, that she had concocted.

Enough of this endless agonizing, she chided herself. Her decision was made when she chose to meet Matt. Lauren was going to marry the man. Unless he backed out—and there seemed to be no chance of that now—she would be Matt Kennerly's wife.

''Oh, I forgot.'' He set his briefcase down on the bench beside them and fished in his pocket, taking out a small, black velvet box. ''Here.'' He casually handed the tiny case to Lauren. ''If you don't like it, we can exchange it for another one.''

She opened the box carefully. Inside was a large, emerald-cut diamond solitaire. The ring was beautiful in its simplicity. Under normal circumstances she would have been delighted with it. But somehow the picture was wrong. Was it the setting—the lobby of a municipal building—that bothered her, or the fact that Matt acted as if the ring was just another item on his to-do list for the day?

''What did you expect, dummy?'' she muttered. ''You advertised for business, not romance.''

''Did you say something?''

''I was just wondering, uh, whenever did you have time to buy it?''

Matt chuckled. "Would you believe I ran, literally, from my office to Neiman Marcus, charged in just as it opened, grabbed the ring, jumped on a Hop-a-Bus coming back and was in the courtroom at ten twenty-nine for my ten-thirty appointment?"

"I'd just as likely believe you sent your secretary out for it on her coffee break."

"Skeptical lady, aren't you? Well, for your information, I don't have my secretary taking care of my personal business. Now quit being suspicious and put it on."

Lauren slipped the ring onto her finger.

"So do you like it?" he prodded.

"What's not to like? I'll be the envy of half the women in Dallas. The diamond must be four carats."

"Four and a half."

Lauren glanced at the ring. "I stand corrected." Why such a big stone? she wondered. Because he wanted to look good in front of his friends and acquaintances, that was why. Oh well, the people she knew would be impressed too. She just prayed no one, outside of Casey, would ever learn the truth about this marriage.

"Okay." Matt reached for her elbow. "That's one chore out of the way." He was steering her toward the elevator. "Now let's get going." He took her elbow. "First the license, then a quick lunch. I have to be back at the courthouse by two."

Lauren held back. "Why do we have to get the license now? What's the big hurry?"

He managed to get her inside the elevator, the doors closing in front of them as he pushed a button to select a floor before he answered her. "I said I wanted to get married right away and you agreed, Lauren. So what's wrong?"

"It's so quick. I was just trying to get used to being engaged," she protested. "In fact, we've probably rushed that a bit. Why don't we take things a little slower, perhaps wait a month or so before we marry?"

"Well, maybe you're right. Maybe we should take this slower. Wait on the marriage—move in together and do a trial run. Sample the wares, so to speak."

"You're impossible!"

"We should see if we're compatible."

"I'm beginning to think we're not one bit compatible," she snapped. "Let's just forget the whole thing." Lauren moved toward the elevator buttons, trying to find one to stop the car at the next floor so she could get off. She accidentally pushed emergency stop and the car jerked to a standstill. "That's great. Now look what you made me do!"

"I'm sorry." He stroked a finger down the side of her cheek. "I shouldn't have teased you. It's just that I thought we'd been all through this last night. All our reasons for marriage are legitimate." He got down on one knee and grabbed her hand. "Lauren, will you marry me? Will you marry me right away? This week?" He began kissing her hand.

"Okay, okay." She laughed. "I give up."

He stood up. "Great." Then he gave her a tender kiss and said softly, "I'll make you very glad you did."

His gentle words mesmerized her. Fortunately they were alone in the elevator, although Lauren doubted she would have noticed anyone else anyway. What was he doing to her? This wasn't the kind of proposal she thought she wanted, yet he made it sound so wonderful . . . and not one bit like a business arrangement.

"This is the way I see it. We get the license now and in a few days we run by one of the judge's chambers, and voilà, you're Lauren Kennerly, or Grayson-Kennerly, or whatever. No fuss, no sweat." He took her chin in his hand and tilted her head toward his. "And if you don't like that idea, then we could just elope. Would that be more appealing?"

She shook her head. "No, we can't marry in a judge's chambers and we can't elope. It just won't work. We'll have to have some sort of a real wedding."

"Oh, gone conventional on me, have you?" Matt touched his hand to his forehead in feigned surprise. "You want white lace and orange blossoms?"

"No, that's not it—it's my family. They would never understand if they weren't included in my wedding."

"You're probably right. So in three days we'll have a simple ceremony and include all your family."

"But there's so much to be done."

"I said simple. We won't be competing with British royalty, will we? No gold coaches or military escorts on horseback?"

"No way," she agreed. "After five stints as a bridesmaid, I view a large wedding as something akin to a three-ring circus."

"That's settled then." He released the emergency stop button and the elevator continued its ascent. They got off and entered the small marriage-license bureau. In response to a signal from a clerk, Matt steered Lauren to a desk by the window. He motioned her to sit down in one of the two chairs facing the desk, but she shook her head, moving to look out the window instead.

"She's a little nervous." Matt winked at the clerk and got a laugh in return.

"It happens sometimes," the woman said, pulling out a set of forms and handing them to Matt to complete. "Just a few vital statistics."

Matt glanced at the forms, then pulled a pen from his jacket pocket. "What's your middle name?" He directed his question at Lauren's back.

"Christine," she answered without turning.

"Hmm. Nice. When's your birthday?"

The clerk looked puzzled. "It doesn't sound like you've known each other very long." She watched warily as Matt continued filling out the forms.

"Oh, Lauren," he asked, again winking at the clerk, "you haven't been divorced within the past thirty days, have you? We can't get married if you have."

Lauren turned and frowned at him. "I sure wouldn't be leaping into marriage again if I had just been divorced. This one experience has been bad enough."

Matt shook his head, looking as if he were totally perplexed by her attitude. "You're the one who suggested marriage—and now you act like I'm tricking you into something. Quit complaining and sign here."

Lauren glanced at the clerk. The woman was studying them as though they'd just come in from another planet. She gave the clerk an embarrassed smile, then moved to the desk and signed her name. She could understand the clerk's attitude—she herself was beginning to feel like a participant in a Three Stooges comedy. Yet she was going through the motions as though they all made sense.

Matt took the form from her and with a flourish signed his name, then pulled out his wallet. It was empty. "Do you have any cash, babe? I've only got some credit cards."

Lauren opened her purse and took out a ten and a twenty. Not only had she agreed to marry this idiot, she thought, she'd just picked up the tab for the marriage license. And what was this "babe" bit? She wasn't sure she liked the endearment. Still, for some weird reason Lauren felt happy—anxious, but happy. She shook her head as though to clear the cobwebs.

They left the Records Building, license in hand, and walked the few blocks to a Chinese restaurant in the West End.

The waiter took their order and brought them tall glasses of iced tea with lemon. The traditional hot Chinese tea was out of the question on this steamy hundred-degree summer day. Lauren pulled a tissue from her purse and dabbed at the perspiration on her forehead. All this rushing around had unsettled her. Silly girl, she told herself, it wasn't just the rushing around. She'd felt restless since the first morning she'd met Matt Kennerly. She needed to get things back in hand, to feel in control of her life again. She played with her teaspoon as she posed a question to Matt. "How would you feel about a pre-nuptial agreement?"

"What for?" Matt's dark eyebrows met. "I know I don't have that much to protect. Have you got a big trust fund I don't know about? Or maybe a handsome dowry?"

"No dowry." Lauren laughed nervously. "It's not that. It's just that I understand it's the thing to do these days."

Matt's eyes turned devilish. "Well, we sure don't want to miss doing 'the thing,' do we?" he said dryly. He pulled out a ballpoint pen and began writing on the pink linen napkin. "Let's see. I'll do the dishes on Monday, Wednesday and Friday. You'll handle them on Tuesday, Thursday and Saturday. On Sunday, we'll eat on paper plates. I'll take out the garbage, you'll feed the cat...."

"I'm sure you realize I was thinking more in terms of how we'll split expenses, whether we'll have a joint checking account—you know, the business details."

"Okay." He picked up his pen. "You bought the marriage license, I'll pay for lunch." He scribbled on the napkin as he talked.

"Matt, I'm serious."

"So am I. If you think we need a legal document, I have lots of experience in putting them together. But, business arrangement aside, I was hoping for a little trust in our relationship." He paused, eyeing the waiter as he placed some spring rolls in front of them. "People like us don't need written contracts. Couldn't we just shake on it? Or better still, considering the type of agreement we're entering into, maybe we'd better kiss on it." He took a bite of his spring roll.

Matt acted as if the discussion was closed, but Lauren wasn't ready to give in so easily. "Okay, so forget the written agreement," she said. "But there are still some matters I think we should discuss. For instance, we haven't even talked about where we're going to live."

"You mean like my place or yours?"

"Something like that."

"All right—how about your place for a while? It's nicer than mine. Then, later if you want, we'll start house hunting. Maybe the professional decorator would enjoy a turn at her own house?"

Lauren was surprised at the feeling of pleasure that surged through her. "Yes, I might like that," she admitted.

"Okay. That's settled, except for one thing." He grinned. "What size bed do you have?"

"Uh . . . a king."

"Good. I can't stand cramped beds. We don't have to worry about buying a new one, then."

"Oh."

Matt smiled. "You should see the funny expression on your face, and I do believe you're blushing. Lauren, you did intend to let me share your bed, didn't you?"

"Well, I..." Her mouth was open, but her brain seemed to be on hold and she stopped in mid-sentence.

"All along we've talked about a normal marriage—no tricks, no subterfuge. You said you wanted a home and family, isn't that right?"

"Yes."

"So, I suppose that means we'll have a normal marriage—in every way. Do I make myself clear?"

"Perfectly," Lauren answered, grateful that the waiter had arrived with the rest of their lunch.

Obligingly Matt changed the subject and Lauren listened as he described his ranch in East Texas. It was a small place he had dubbed the Ponderosa, and was just over two hours from the city. They would be able to drive there easily after the wedding ceremony and not be travel weary. Lauren was pleased Matt had made no jesting comments about a honeymoon; his earlier statements had been enough.

Just thinking about consummating their marriage made her nervous—yet excited, too. But she felt awkward discussing the subject. Well, she wouldn't have to think about it for the time being as there was no more time to linger, anyway. Matt's next appointment was near at hand. He summoned the waiter for the check. It arrived with two fortune cookies.

"Look at this," Matt laughed. "'Stick strictly to business and you'll be rewarded.' I'm looking forward to my reward. What does yours say?"

"'Watch out for those who would take advantage of you,'" Lauren improvised, crumpling the paper that actually read, "Love is closer than you think," and dropping it into a small dish holding the cookie bits.

"Not to worry," Matt said. "I'll protect you from predators."

Yes, Lauren thought, *but who'll protect me from you?*

They walked back to Lauren's car and she bade Matt goodbye. "Enjoyed our lunch," he said, grabbing her hand firmly and giving it an exaggerated pumping. "Nice doing business with you." He turned and headed toward the courthouse.

Lauren watched him go. She didn't know whether to be irritated or amused at his flippancy. He had certainly managed to undermine any of the romantic aspects of the past few hours, scanty though they might have been. "You sap," she said to herself. "Just remember what this is all about—a business arrangement. Quit looking for more."

"YOU WHAT?"

"You heard me," Lauren said. "I agreed to marry him."

Casey dropped the brochures she was holding onto the floor. She picked them up and set them on the counter, then walked over to Lauren. She placed a hand on Lauren's forehead. "No temperature. I guess you aren't delirious with fever."

"Please, Casey. I'm not delirious at all."

"Well, you've certainly done an about-face. We're talking about a person you couldn't stand a few days ago."

"I guess he just grows on you," Lauren answered weakly.

"Grows on you? You make him sound like a fungus." Casey shook her head smiling. "The man's got to have more to him than parasite appeal for you just to up and decide to marry him. I mean other than the obvious—the gorgeous bod, the sexy bedroom eyes, the charm, the charisma... Say, what am I doing, trying to discourage you. You'd better grab him while you can. Heaven knows there aren't too many good ones left. Believe me, I'm an expert."

"So you're with me?" Lauren gave a tentative smile.

"Of course, I'm with you. Other than being insanely jealous of what you've got, I'm very happy for you." Casey wrapped her arms around Lauren in a warm hug. "In fact, this might be a good time for a confession...."

"Oh?"

"I wasn't going to tell you this. I didn't want to get my head chewed off. You remember our conversations about the ad—my telling you it was a stupid idea?"

Lauren nodded.

"Well, since you were so gung ho on going against my good advice, I decided to liven things up a bit. I'm the one who sent you the response with Matt's card."

"What?" Lauren was flabbergasted.

"Now don't get mad. My intentions were good. I was just trying to make things a little more interesting, that's all. Look at the responses you got on your own—Rex and George." Casey rolled her eyes to the ceiling.

"I can't believe my ears. My partner, my best friend, setting me up for one of the most embarrassing moments of my life!"

"All right, all right, I know I was wrong. I'm sorry for that. But you wouldn't be marrying this guy if it weren't for what I did. Just don't forget that."

"Oh, no. You're not going to get off the hook that easily." Lauren shook her head. "I deserve a complete explanation before I decide whether to move you onto my ex-friends list.''

"Okay, I'll explain. Only there's not that much more to tell. When I knew you were actually going through with this classified ad stunt, I decided it would be great if you met someone terrific. So I tried to make that happen.''

"By foisting me off on Matt?''

"Exactly.''

"But why Matt, and how...?''

"A few weeks ago I was working out at the spa and one of the women there was telling me about her lawyer. She said he'd just handled her divorce and how wonderful, how gorgeous, he was—and sexy. So I sorta fibbed to her and said a close friend was looking for a good divorce lawyer, and she whips this card out of her purse. It was Matt's—I think you can figure out the rest.''

"Yes, I guess I can.''

"So, are you terribly mad?''

Lauren paused for a few seconds, then smiled. "Well, I suppose I have you to thank for this.'' She held out her hand to show Casey the engagement ring.

"Wow! Now I know you can't be mad.''

"Maybe not. But remember—if things don't work out, I know who to blame.''

"Okay, but if they do work out, I intend to be repaid with introductions to every one of Matt's single friends.''

"Deal.''

"So tell me, how did your parents take all this?''

"Well, actually, they don't know yet. I was trying it out on you first.''

Casey put a hand to her face. "And you were worried about my reaction? I can hear your father bellowing now. Your mother—she'll be thrilled. After all, she's been waiting for this day since you were sixteen. But your father? Lyle Grayson's not going to be too pleased to discover his daughter's running away with a guy on the second date and getting married.'' Casey's eyes widened as though a light had gone on in her brain. "They don't know about the ad, do they?"

"Hardly,'' Lauren said defensively. "And anyway, we've had three dates, not two. And tonight will make the fourth when we go by and tell the folks.''

"There may not be a fifth after your father finishes with Matt.''

"Don't be silly. Daddy knows Matt. And likes him.''

"Well, he's going to have to like him a whole lot to let him take off with his little girl—just like that.''

"He does,'' Lauren said. "Believe me, he does.'' She looked around her desk. "Now where's my appointment book? I have some major rescheduling to do. Then I have to call my mother and tell her to expect company this evening.''

THE DOORBELL RANG, just as Matt had promised it would, at seven sharp. He stood there with a single long-stemmed red rose in one hand and his watch in the other. "On the dot,'' he said, holding out the watch to show her the time. "I've been standing here for six minutes waiting for the assigned hour. Am I forgiven for being late this morning?"

"You idiot.'' She accepted the rose. "Quite forgiven.''

He pulled her against him and gave her a long hungry kiss. "I've missed you,'' he said, as his lips reluctantly released hers.

"Already? You saw me only a few hours ago.'' What was he up to now with the floral offering and the generous words? She'd seen glimpses of this charming side of his nature before, and it disturbed her almost as much as his bullheadedness. It made her feel all sappy and giddy, as if she no longer had control of her senses.

"You're like Chinese food," he said. "A couple of hours later I'm ready for more."

She gave a playful laugh as she closed the door and followed him to the living room. If he wanted to play Prince Charming tonight she'd go along with him. "I'm not sure whether or not to take that as a compliment," she flirted, her brown eyes sparkling.

"Oh, it's a compliment," he assured her. He reached for her again, and his lips came down on hers, more ardently than the first time. This time he did not release her.

Lauren eventually pushed him away. "Please, Matt," she gasped. "No more."

"I was just sealing our agreement." He pulled his head back, his eyes twinkling questioningly. "Sure you want to wait for the honeymoon?"

Lauren could feel her pulse accelerate. "My parents are expecting us in fifteen minutes," she managed to say.

Matt released her and gave a rueful smile. "Well, that's one good way to cool a guy's ardor. Tell him he's about to face the music." He nuzzled her hair. "But I know it'll eventually be worth it. I'm counting the minutes until I can hold you—really hold you." He sighed loudly. "But let's go get this over with first."

A short time later they stood on the front steps of the imposing Grayson house. Matt pressed the doorbell and they waited silently until the door opened.

"Lauren. Matt. Come in." Lyle Grayson shook Matt's hand. "Good to see you again." He gave Lauren a quick embrace and gestured them down the long hall toward the French doors at the back of the house. "Jeanette's waiting for us out on the patio with her special sangria. Hope you two are thirsty.''

"Very thirsty,'' Matt answered. The tone of his voice caused Lauren to look his way. Was the formidable Matthew Kennerly nervous? Surely not. She didn't think anything could disturb Matt.

"I was surprised when your mother said you'd called about coming over tonight—it was the first I'd heard that you and Matt were dating. Of course she's delighted—she thought she'd detected sparks between the two of you.''

"There were certainly sparks from the beginning,'' Matt agreed, smiling.

Jeanette Grayson rose from the white, wrought-iron chair to greet her daughter and Matt, hugging them both. "It's so pleasant this evening I thought we'd just sit outside.'' Jeanette motioned the three of them to join her at the glass-topped patio table. She picked up the large pitcher of sangria, filled with sliced oranges and limes, and poured generous glassfuls for each of them.

Lauren hoped there was enough red wine in the drink to soothe the tension in her shoulders. After what Casey had said about her father, she'd begun to dread the task that lay ahead. She glanced at Matt and noticed him clench his jaw a couple of times. So he *was* nervous. Lauren felt an odd sense of satisfaction.

The foursome spent the next several minutes making chitchat. Lauren wondered how she and Matt were going to broach the subject of their marriage. She regretted now that the two of them hadn't spent some time plotting their strategy beforehand. Matt gave her a quick questioning glance, and she shot back a look intended to convey an I-don't-know response. More idle conversation ensued. Jeanette poured another round of the red punch.

Finally Lauren could stand the tension no longer. "Mother, Daddy. Matt and I have something to tell you."

"Oh?" Jeanette Grayson's head jerked toward her daughter. Her probing look told Lauren she knew something was up.

"We intend to marry." She pulled her left hand out of the pocket of her dress and placed it on the table.

"My goodness." Jeanette stared at the ring. "This is quite a surprise."

"I should say so," Lyle chimed in. Both he and his wife studied the ring, then exchanged long glances, neither revealing their thoughts to Lauren or Matt, but rather passing silent messages to each other, in the way only long-time married people can.

Jeanette picked up Lauren's hand and examined the ring closely. "It's beautiful, darling." She smiled, then a look of concern crossed her face. "I always knew when you found the right man it'd be quick—like fireworks exploding. Still, it does seem so sudden...."

"We know it's a shock—and, yes, it is sudden, but it's what we want."

"Well," Lyle said, "your mother and I would be the last ones to stand in the way of young love."

"But we're really going to have our work cut out for us getting the wedding planned," Jeanette said. "There's so much to take care of. We've got to call the boys and get them and Melissa and Dee over here to help work up a guest list. When do you plan to marry—in the winter? Or maybe next spring?"

"This week," Matt answered. "We plan to marry this week."

"Oh, my!" Jeanette's response this time was a gasp. "Surely there's no reason to rush so." Lyle and Jeanette were looking from Lauren to Matt and back again, obviously expecting an answer.

Matt stepped into the fray, as if he was soothing a presiding judge. "Now that we've finally found each other, we don't want to wait. Anyway," he said with a laugh, "it took some convincing to get Lauren to say yes. I sure don't want to give her time to change her mind."

Jeanette and Lyle laughed, too. "But there are so many details," Jeanette fretted. "I don't think I could pull a wedding together so quickly. There's the cake, the invitations, the guests, the florist.... We probably couldn't even get the church scheduled on such short notice."

Lauren placed her hands on her mother's. "It's not going to be that kind of wedding. We want a simple little ceremony here at the house. Just the family, and Casey of course. And that's all. Nothing fancy."

"But Lauren," Jeanette protested, "what about all our friends and neighbors, your father's business associates—we just can't leave everyone out."

"Matt and I have talked it over, Mother. Daddy..." Lauren's eyes pleaded for Lyle's support.

"Maybe we could compromise," he suggested. "How about a small wedding—then a real blowout, a slambang, no-expenses-spared party later on?"

"I don't have a problem with that." Lauren looked at Matt.

"Okay with me," he agreed. "After the honeymoon."

"Mother?" Lauren looked at Jeanette.

Jeanette nodded.

"Well, I'm glad that's settled." Lyle rose from his chair. His face showed a slight flush. "Matt, I think you know I've always had a lot of respect for you. But I have to admit this announcement has been a bit of a surprise—I didn't think we'd be planning a wedding to-night." He pulled a handkerchief from his pocket and wiped it across his forehead. "I didn't even realize you and Lauren knew each other until that dinner here at the house. Just how long have you been acquainted?"

Lauren could see a hint of red on Matt's neck. His Adam's apple bobbed as he took a deep swallow. "I'm sure you wouldn't think it's long enough, sir."

Lauren breathed a sigh of relief. That had been the perfect answer. She heard a deep, rumbling laugh come from Lyle's lips. "Sir?" He laughed again. "I guess I'd forgotten what a chore this can be." He picked up his empty glass and passed it to his wife for a refill. "Jeanette, remember when we went to see your parents about getting married?"

"How could I forget? It's become a family joke."

"We were young—Jeanette only eighteen. I went over for dinner, as nervous as a calf at branding time. Doug, Jeanette's younger brother, was about thirteen at the time. We were eating steak, and in my dither I was apparently really shoving it in because Doug said, 'Gee, Lyle, you really like steak, don't you?'" Lyle took the filled glass from Jeanette and took a sip. "I was so embarrassed, I put down my fork and didn't take another bite. After dinner, I had to go into the parlor for a heart-to-heart talk with her father. Matt, be glad the ritual of asking the bride's father for his daughter's hand in marriage is a thing of the past."

"I'd be willing to go through that—if that's what it took to get your blessing."

Lauren frowned. *Cool it,* she thought. *Don't lay it on too thick.*

"I'm sure you would," she heard her father answer. "So will you step into the parlour, please?" he kidded, then extended a hand across the table. "Welcome to the family."

Matt rose to accept the handshake. "Thanks, Lyle." He shot a mischievous wink at Jeanette and Lauren. "Or should I make that 'Dad'?"

"Call me Dad and I'll have your hide nailed to the wall of my office," Lyle snorted. He stared at his glass of sangria. "Come on into the den. I think I need a real drink about now. And I'll bet you do, too. That'll give these ladies some time to put their heads together."

"That's a great idea." Matt followed Lyle into the house.

CHAPTER FIVE

LAUREN SLUMPED into her desk chair, exhausted—as if she'd been run over by a truck. She examined her slouched body. No, no tread marks. Must just be the residue from the hectic pace of the past couple of days. Perhaps it was fortunate Matt had wanted to get married right away. Lauren didn't think she could survive a long engagement. What with trying to get the loose ends tied up at the office and talking to her mother on the telephone every few hours, she hadn't had a moment to spare.

"I've just finished with the Parkers." Casey entered her office and sat down beside her desk. "We're redoing their guest house. Remember that pastel color scheme?"

Lauren nodded. "Glad you're getting some work done. I've really slacked off this week. But I'll make up for it. Not today, though. Do you still have time for some shopping?"

"You know me," answered Casey, who was indefatigable in a shopping mall. She even had a shirt with a slogan that read born to shop. "Let's get going."

An hour or so later, Lauren tugged at the zipper and started taking off the pink lace dress. "I don't know when I've had so much trouble making up my mind," she moaned. "I guess this dress is as good as any. I have to buy something. It's almost noon and the wedding's tomorrow."

"Well, you two shouldn't have been so impatient."

"Matt wasn't willing to wait. I think he wants to get the wedding over with so we can get on with our lives."

"Are you sure that's why he's impatient?" Casey teased. "For someone who didn't want a wife a few weeks ago, he's certainly chomping at the bit for one right now."

Lauren would just as soon not talk about Matt's haste, especially in relationship to his previous hesitancy. She had enough doubts—concerns she pushed into her subconscious—without Casey adding to them. Lauren had wavered back and forth long enough. Her decision had been made.

She slipped on her blouse and skirt. "I'll take the pink lace," she told the salesclerk who had just stuck her head in the door.

"What about a hat?" Casey asked.

"Oh, I think I'd rather wear fresh flowers in my hair. Where to next?" she asked Casey, who held Lauren's hand-written shopping list.

Four stores and one cafeteria later they were back in front of Classic Interiors, Lauren's car laden with her wedding dress and matching shoes, a swimsuit, sandals, two new sundresses, and several pairs of shorts with matching tops. She had also bought two nightgowns, a light summer robe and a complete wardrobe of frilly, feminine lingerie—all the while trying to ignore Casey's good-natured teasing. Casey had added a white silk tissue-paper-thin negligee to Lauren's purchases, calling it a wedding present.

"Not that you'll need this night stuff," Casey said with a smirk. "But I guess it's all part of the trousseau tradition."

"I'm afraid I've still got a million things to do." Lauren studied the list, ignoring Casey's gibing. She didn't want to talk about that aspect of the marriage. Matt's comments had been embarrassing enough. Even though there was a definite sexual attraction between them, the whole idea of making love with him unsettled her.

Casey climbed out of the car. "Bye now. Try to get to bed early—you'll be needing your rest, what with that gorgeous hunk of male to deal with after the wedding."

Lauren wadded up a sales receipt and tossed it at Casey through the open window. "See you tomorrow," she said as her friend retrieved the paper from the ground.

"Tomorrow," Casey answered, dropping the sales receipt back into the car. "And remember to toss your bridal bouquet just the same way—in my direction."

Lauren drove through the late-afternoon traffic, the long delays giving her time to think—too much time. Her mind kept going back to her earlier concerns. She was actually going to marry a man who had thrown her out of his office at their first meeting. A man she'd known only slightly more than two weeks. A man who'd never uttered words of love, or devotion.

For what must have been the hundredth time, Lauren reviewed the reasons she had placed the ad. They were no less valid today than they had been a month ago. She wanted a marriage based on respect, responsibility, mutual goals. A desire for home and children. But could Matt really feel the same way? He said he did. So why did she feel so unsure? She wished he hadn't taken off on that business trip to San Antonio right after they'd talked to her parents. She needed his strong reassurance. Maybe she'd feel less hesitant if he'd been around these past few days.

Their whirlwind engagement could probably make *The Guinness Book of Records* for lack of romance—an engagement ring presented in a government building, then the groom leaving town until the day of the wedding. Still, Matt had performed some of the niceties of courtship—being charming and attentive in front of her family, sending flowers. He'd even called her twice from San Antonio. But their conversations had been perfunctory, obligatory, with no whispered words of love. "Is that what you want...*love*?" Lauren admonished herself aloud. "Well, that wasn't included in the deal."

She pulled into a shopping center and parked in front of the grocery store. She needed more food for Pandora and a few other little things.

Lauren took a grocery cart and started crisscrossing the aisles. She grabbed cat food, some shampoo and two cartons of yogurt. Was this the way she would shop after she and Matt were married? Or would she be heading for the gourmet section looking for tempting goodies with which to entice her husband? Would marriage change her?

She recalled her friend Sandra, who'd gone through several marriages and divorces, saying that marriage changes a woman—that she becomes dependent, clingy. Lauren was determined this wouldn't happen to her. That would be one of the advantages to the relationship she and Matt had planned—they would remain their own persons.

LAUREN SIPPED HER CHOCOLATE instant breakfast to the accompaniment of birds chirping in the tree outside the kitchen window. It was just growing light, but she could already tell that the day was going to be bright and sunny.

A good omen for a wedding, she thought, ignoring the fact that most summer days in Dallas were sunny.

Her wedding day—it was hard to believe. Matt had wanted the ceremony to take place the day before, but Jeanette Grayson had won an extra twenty-four hours. And that was fortunate, Lauren decided, as she'd needed the additional time to clear up loose ends at the office, and Matt had to finish his business in south Texas. With both of them so busy, her mother had taken it upon herself to telephone an ever-enlarging list of guests, which had grown from the immediate family and Casey, a gathering of less than ten, to, at last count, some sixty-five people. It was just as well Matt had no close relatives. There would be no space in the living room for anyone else.

"Give your mother one more day and we'll need Texas Stadium for the ceremony," Matt had quipped on the telephone the night before.

Lauren laughed. "It's not that bad."

"Oh no? I thought by our agreeing to a post-honeymoon party, we'd avoid all this. What in heaven's name is she going to do for an encore?"

"Don't ask. Just don't ask," Lauren replied. "In this case, you're better off not knowing."

LAUREN ENTERED the Grayson home, her suitcase in one hand and the wedding dress, in a plastic garment bag, over her other arm. Matt had a point, she decided, as she surveyed the chaotic scene. She hoped he wouldn't hit the ceiling when he saw things spinning out of control.

The house was a hub of activity—the florist in one room, the people from the rental company in another; there was even a crew cleaning the windows. Greenery draped the fireplace, and flower arrangements and candelabra were set up at each end of the mantel. A white satin kneeler lay in front of the fireplace. All the living-room furniture, except the grand piano, had been removed, and rows of blue metal folding chairs were now in place.

Lauren set the suitcase down, draped the garment bag over a chair and sighed. She really couldn't be angry with her mother for going overboard. Jeanette had no idea that romance wasn't the key ingredient in Matt's and Lauren's relationship. And after all, this was her first—and, she hoped, only—chance to play mother of the bride. When her sons were married, she'd just had to sit back and let someone else run the show. Even worse, she'd had to follow the old mandate for mother of the groom: "wear beige and keep your mouth shut." A difficult task for Jeanette Grayson.

"Mother, are you here?" Lauren called.

"Oh, darling, I'm so glad you're early." Jeanette rushed in from the dining room. "Come look at the cake."

Lauren followed her mother back into the dining room. A three-tiered wedding cake topped by the traditional bride and groom sat in the middle of the table, flanked by a silver punch bowl and a smaller chocolate groom's cake. Rita was at the buffet, arranging fancy dessert plates, silver forks, and a stack of paper napkins with the imprint Lauren and Matt, around a floral centerpiece. She looked up and smiled at Lauren, then disappeared into the kitchen for another stack of plates.

"Do you think cake, punch and champagne will be enough, dear?" Jeanette was obviously worried. "I really should have planned some canapés, and maybe some pâté."

"This is perfect, Mother," Lauren comforted. "Matt and I didn't want a big to-do, remember? And we'll be leaving soon after the ceremony."

"Well—if you're sure."

"I'm positive." Lauren was feeling more and more like a fraud. Matt had had the right idea after all; a basic no-frills quickie ceremony. It probably would have been easier on everyone just to head for Las Vegas and tie the knot, some thousand miles away from her family and their fantasies. Lauren hoped she and Matt would be able to act the part of normal newlyweds. She didn't want to disappoint her family. "I love the wedding cake," she gushed, trying to sound sincere. "How did you manage to get such a gorgeous one so fast?"

Jeanette laughed. "I told the bakery they owed it to me with all the business I've given them over the years." She hesitated. "And, of course, I slipped them a big fat tip."

"Well, everything looks terrific." She hugged her mother. "Thank you for all your work."

"I've loved every minute of it. Thank you and Matt for letting me have my way a little with all this. Now you'd better run upstairs and start getting ready. Gary is going to be over in about an hour to do your hair—you've just got time for a nice, relaxing bubble bath."

Lauren picked up her dress, grabbed the suitcase she'd left in the foyer and headed up the circular stairs. Although she'd moved away from home after college, her mother still kept her old room intact, as she did for her brothers. Lauren sat on her old bed and thought for a moment about her parents and how lucky she was. Lyle and Jeanette had always been so caring, so devoted to their family. Matt's life, as he described it, had been different—an only child of divorced parents, now deceased. Had he missed the give and take, the togetherness, of a big family? Was this one of the reasons for his eagerness to marry her?

"Mother!" She jumped up and rushed to Jeanette, who came in holding an antique satin wedding gown.

"Well—does it make you happy?" Jeanette hung the dress on the back of the closet door.

Lauren hugged her mother, then brushed a tear from her eye. "It definitely makes me happy." She fingered the smooth fabric of the heirloom, its color aged to a soft ivory. The dress had belonged to her grandmother, then passed down to Jeanette, and had been worn by Melissa and Dee, also. One of Lauren's major regrets about this arranged marriage was that she wouldn't be wearing the dress. "This is wonderful. But will it fit?"

"You and Melissa are the same size. She wore it last. Except you're a little taller of course. I had some lace added to cover the line where we let the hem down. You're the tallest bride yet."

"Do you realize how many stores I went to yesterday looking for something to wear?" Lauren gestured toward the garment bag lying on the bed.

Jeanette went over and pulled the plastic cover off the pink lace dress. "Very pretty—it wasn't time wasted. This will be perfect for your party. I bet you forgot all about shopping for that."

"As a matter of fact, I did," Lauren admitted. "Everything's happened so fast I can't seem to concentrate on more than one thing at a time."

AT ONE O'CLOCK the pianist began playing Mendelssohn's *Wedding March*. As Lauren made her way down the spiral stairs, with her father by her side, she saw Matt for the first time in days. He was standing next to her brothers—he had asked them to share the best-man duties. Casey, the maid of honor, was waiting on the opposite side of the fireplace. But Lauren's eyes were glued to the man she had agreed to marry.

The sight of him took her breath away. He was wearing a blue suit with a crisp white shirt, and a blue-and-burgundy silk tie. Lauren faltered a moment, feeling overwhelmed by what was happening. As he saw her, Matt's face showed surprise, then his expression changed to one of solemnity. He looked more like a condemned felon than a groom. Had he changed his mind? Was he there only out of duty, to honor an ill-conceived promise?

Lauren felt like beating a retreat upstairs. Then Matt's eyes caught hers and held them, pulling her toward him, blocking out everyone else in the room, and any second thoughts she might be having about this wedding.

"Repeat after me," the minister intoned. "I, Matthew Creighton Kennerly, take thee, Lauren Christine Grayson, to be my lawful wedded wife...."

Matt's voice rang out firm and clear. Lauren's response was softer, but no less sure. Her right hand was firmly held in Matt's and she continued to gaze into his eyes, eyes now soft as gray velvet.

The ceremony seemed almost unreal. Lauren had tried to think of the actual nuptials as just another detail necessary to effect their agreement. Instead she was full of emotion—she felt tearful, but excited and anticipatory too, feelings she hadn't expected. What was happening to her? She was in a dreamlike state when Matt's warm, sure lips met hers to seal their vows.

"IF WE GO through many more toasts, I'm not going to be able to drive to Jefferson," Matt protested in an aside to Lauren about half an hour after the ceremony. It was the first effort he'd made to talk to her—or any one else, as far as Lauren had noticed, since the ceremony. For the most part Matt had been surprisingly serious. A little obligatory joking with her brothers—that had been it. Lauren doubted anyone else had noticed, but under the circumstances, she couldn't help feeling disturbed and uneasy about his behavior. He sure wasn't playing the role of the proud groom.

"At least the toasts have been short and sweet," she responded, trying to lighten his mood. "Casey's should be the last."

Casey raised her champagne glass. "I know these two are ready to run out on us, so I'll make this brief—to Lauren, Matt, and a free press."

The crowd looked at Casey a bit strangely but obediently raised their glasses. "I think that's our cue to exit," Matt said. "Before anyone asks for clarification. Are you ready to go?"

"I'll need about five minutes to change," she answered.

A few minutes later they paused at the front door to bid farewell to the family and remaining guests. Lauren glanced Casey's way, turned and tossed her bouquet. The flowers sailed over her head, but Casey made a grandstand catch, and while the group's attention was directed her way, Lauren and Matt made their getaway. They were only steps ahead of a shower of rice—not far enough away to avoid getting some of the good-luck charm on their hair and clothing.

"Where's the nearest car wash?" Matt groused as he spotted his car, decorated with pink and blue crepe-paper streamers and balloons. Tin cans were strung from the back bumper and baby bootees dangled from the antenna. White shoe polish had been used to paint a few not-so-cryptic messages on the windows and back wind-shield. A big white heart had been drawn on the driver's side. Lauren held her breath as Matt stared at the car, then she sighed in relief as his sense of humor finally surfaced and he laughed.

"You might as well get used to them—after all, they are your brothers-in-law."

"Don't remind me," he grumbled good-naturedly. He opened the door for Lauren, then returned to his side and climbed in.

Lyle Grayson bent to speak to them through the window. "Drive carefully, you two. And, Matt, take care of my little girl."

After a detour through a car wash, Lauren and Matt were cruising down Interstate 20 on their way to East Texas. The landscape slowly changed from prairie to pine as the miles ticked off. The roadsides were dotted with tall evergreens, and in the clearings every few miles, were small homesteads with tiny ponds. The Texas trade-marks of oil and cattle were abundantly evident, with livestock grazing in open fields and oil derricks visible from the highway. One roadside park even displayed small reproductions of the derricks as decorative crown-ing for the picnic tables.

The couple had spoken few words during the trip, each seemingly lost in thought. Finally Matt broke the si-lence. "You looked very virginal today."

His tone of voice reminded Lauren of the one he'd used in his office the first day they met, and it made her uncomfortable.

"Well, are you . . ."

She didn't reply.

". . . virginal?"

"Are you?" she snapped.

Matt smiled, seemingly pleased to have evoked an angry response from her. "I'll let you judge for yourself a little later."

Matt turned off the interstate onto a state highway, and then a few miles later exited onto a narrow, curving farm road. The scenery here was bucolic and beautiful, thick and lush. The stately pines signalled the beginning of the Big Thicket—a splash of forest that ran eastward through the middle of the United States. Lauren loved the pines, so ramrod straight, their long needles a deep rich green. Too bad they didn't grow well in Dallas, she thought.

"Here we are—the Ponderosa," said Matt. "Not quite as big as the one in Bonanza, maybe, but it's mine." He gave her a self-conscious glance. "I guess I should say ours." He drove through an open gate and down a winding drive, which ended in front of a hacienda-style ranch house.

Lauren looked around, impressed by what she saw. The house was just as Matt described it—a rustic two-story building, nestled in trees, the yard enclosed by a wooden fence. White-faced cattle roamed in the distance. Even Lauren, a bona fide city girl, recognized that they were Herefords.

They walked up the wide steps to the ornate front door. Lauren admiringly ran her hand over the intricately carved wood. "It's beautiful," she said. But even her compliment did not ease the strange tension that seemed to have taken over Matt during the ceremony and not abated. He unlocked the door and motioned her inside.

The hallway gleamed of dark polished wood and was flanked by large matching double doors. In the shadows, Lauren could make out a staircase leading to the second floor and behind it another door—probably the kitchen. Matt put down their bags and gestured toward a door on the right.

"Nice," she whispered as she walked across the room to gaze out a large picture window. It framed a lovely view—seemingly endless, pine-sprinkled pasture, several horses lazily grazing in the afternoon sun and a small pond, with a couple of cows on its bank. A peaceful rural scene that Lauren found romantic.

Apparently Lauren wasn't the only one with romantic ideas. She was surprised when she felt Matt's hand gently touch her hair. "It is nice, isn't it?" he said. "I could sit here for hours watching the pond, the cattle... Sometimes I've even seen a deer or two. It's particularly enjoyable on a cold winter evening with a fire roaring." His hand reached for her chin and turned her head to his. His lips met hers, gently, briefly, again and again, showering her with dozens of tiny, teasing kisses. "Let's go upstairs."

"Now?" Talk of an about-face on Matt's part. Suddenly Lauren felt frightened, unsure. For a twenty-nine-year-old, she wasn't very sexually experienced, but she had no doubt Matt was adept, probably an expert. He'd as much as told her so himself. Would she disappoint him? "But it's—"

"It's not even dark, is it?" Matt's irritation was apparent in his voice. "Lauren, that's what this marriage is all about. Surely you realize that." He locked eyes with her.

"About sex?"

"Among other things. We agreed on a normal marriage. Generally newlyweds make love on their honeymoon."

"I realize that. But it's a little difficult to jump into bed with someone who's barely spoken to you since he said I do."

"You weren't very talkative yourself."

"It's hard to have a conversation with a stone wall."

"Stone?" His hands entwined in her hair, then his fingers trickled over her neck and brushed her breasts. "Not stone, Lauren." His lips met hers, gently coaxing a response. His tenderness inflamed her more than any passionate demands could have. He explored her body. He explored her senses. Lauren pressed herself tight against his hard muscular frame. An electrical current charged through her body and she became lost in tumultuous emotion. Matt wrapped an arm around her waist and led her toward the bedroom.

LAUREN RECLINED in a chaise longue as Matt cooked T-bone steaks over the outdoor grill. She could see squirrels frolicking at the edge of the wood, and lightning bugs dancing through the air to the nonstop serenade of cicadas. Matt's wine cellar was small but apparently well stocked—and he saw to it that Lauren's glass was constantly filled. She sipped the delicious burgundy and reflected on the day. Matt had been everything she could ever wish for in a lover—caring, gentle, masterful. Still, she couldn't shed her anxious uncertainty. The mood that had come over Matt at the wedding continued to puzzle her. *Forget it, Lauren,* she scolded herself. *Maybe it was just anxiety. Don't blow it out of proportion. At least he seems content now.*

His voice interrupted her thoughts. "Shall we take these into the house?" He removed the steaks from the grill. "It may be pleasant out here now, but before long we'll be mosquito bait."

She followed him inside and watched as he placed the platter of thick T-bones onto the table, then disappeared into the kitchen and returned with a tossed salad. "Thank goodness one of us can cook," she said.

"Don't get too excited," Matt replied. "Salad and grilled steak are about the extent of my culinary accomplishments."

"We're in trouble," she said. "Big trouble."

After dinner, they moved to the den, the drapes open to the now-darkened scenery. A slice of moon was visible in the sky and millions of stars could be seen over the tops of the trees. With no competition from the neon lights of the city, the stars looked especially clear and bright. Soothing, in a way. She'd been so uptight about their first night together. Fortunately, Matt still seemed to be relaxed, and the evening was going much better than she'd anticipated. Matt was making quite a commendable start as a husband, she decided.

"How did you come to buy this place?" she asked, trying to make light conversation.

"Sort of a fluke," he admitted, motioning her to join him on the couch. "I was representing a client who owned some property in Jefferson. One of those old houses on the national register of historic places." He took a decanter from the coffee table and poured them each a liqueur.

"The main barrier to a divorce settlement between my client and his wife was the house in Jefferson and the poodle—Miss Ellie. I like dogs, so I could understand the competition for the pet, but it took a trip over here to understand why they were fighting about the house."

"So who won?"

"Neither. After months of trying to reach an agreement, the judge finally determined the property should be put on the market and the profits divided. So the house was sold. While I was in the area taking care of the sale, I ran across this place and fell in love with it. I come here every chance I get—I've never regretted the purchase."

"Okay, satisfy my curiosity. Who got the poodle?"

"Joint custody. Six months with one, then the other."

"You're kidding."

"No. Miss Ellie will always have plenty of Kibbles and Bits, and lots of T.L.C." He put his glass down on the coffee table. "And speaking of tender—" he brought his lips to Lauren's neck and brushed a soft kiss on her warm skin "—loving—" his arms moved around her and pulled her body to his "—care..."

THE SOUND OF FOOTSTEPS on the stairs, then the aroma of freshly brewed coffee, preceded Matt as he entered their room and awakened Lauren the next morning. "Coffee, tea or me?" He smiled and placed a tray on the bedside table.

She leaned over to examine the tray. "I don't see any tea," she said, reaching for a cup of coffee.

"Picky, picky. Actually I thought you'd choose me, so I didn't bother with tea." Matt climbed into bed beside her and grabbed a cup for himself. "Want to drive into town for lunch later?" He placed a few short kisses on her cheek. "Hmm...make that much later...."

Matt traced his lips down Lauren's cheeks and neck, his breath warm against her ear. "Lauren, I love..." He hesitated.

She turned her face expectantly toward his.

"I love your body, Lauren."

Lauren felt as if her heart had dropped into her stomach. Had he been going to say "I love you"? No, not

Matt. She dismissed the thought. Matt was always in control; he wouldn't slip up—even in the midst of passion. Besides, even if he did say he loved her, the words didn't necessarily make it so. He could have blurted them out during the heat of the moment. Still it felt so right lying there beside him, her arm resting on his stomach, his arm around her shoulder holding her close.

"I CAN'T BELIEVE you've never been here before." Matt parked his car in front of the Excelsior Hotel.

"Me, neither," Lauren said. "I've wanted to come for a long time."

Jefferson had been a prominent inland port in the past century, but the combined forces of a lowered water level and a vindictive railroad czar had transformed the boomtown into a sleepy village, forgotten for almost a hundred years. Only in the past decade or so had tourism brought this Texas city back to life.

They walked across the redbrick street to the site of Jay Gould's private railroad car, the Atalanta. Gould had been a well-known financier in the nineteenth century. "He was so furious about the Jefferson city fathers not going along with his railroad expansion plans that he angrily wrote 'the end of Jefferson' in the guest register of the Excelsior Hotel and supposedly put a curse on the town." Matt laughed. "Gould must have been quite a character."

"And obviously used to getting his own way," Lauren added. She shook her head in amazement. "His curse seems to have been rather effective."

"Until recently. But you can see all the restoration that's been done. The place is making a comeback."

"Shhh," Lauren said. "You don't want to stir up the curse again."

They crossed back over into the Excelsior and Matt showed Lauren the famous register. They looked with fascination at some of the names entered in it—Ulysses S. Grant, Jacob Astor, even Oscar Wilde, then joined another couple for a tour of the premises.

After leaving the hotel, they walked past antique shops to a small restaurant where they lingered over lunch. There was still time for some window shopping before they headed back to the ranch.

Lauren had felt quite content after the trip. Matt seemed more relaxed than the day before. He'd promised to show her the ranch by horseback and take her fishing in the little pond. She hoped the next few days could be a time of getting to know each other better, sharing memories. Lauren was even beginning to feel as if they could have a real marriage.

But her hope was shattered the moment they returned to the house. The telephone was pealing. Matt had to return to Dallas, then leave immediately to meet a client in Houston. She waited for Matt to tell the client he was unavailable, that business would have to wait until after his honeymoon. She was shocked when he readily agreed to come back. Hurt, but trying not to show it, she hastily threw her belongings into her suitcase and followed Matt to the car.

"I'm sorry," he said, "but there was no getting out of this." She said nothing, averted her eyes from his and climbed into the car. Matt attempted no conversation on the ride back to Dallas and dropped her off at her place without so much as a goodbye kiss. Lauren wasn't to see him again for over a week.

She spent those days trying to convince herself she had no right to feel so abandoned, so annoyed—so just plain angry. After all, she'd taken a private oath to carry on with her life somewhat in the same manner as before, not to make drastic changes simply because she was married. It only made sense that Matt would follow the same plan and have the same privileges. So Lauren decided to go in to the office, to use the time until Matt returned to catch up on the work she'd neglected the past couple of weeks. Casey—romantic that she was—might be upset with her, but Casey knew the terms of her marriage. No need to bring up the fact that Lauren was secretly embarrassed about her honeymoon ending so abruptly. And a part of her kept wondering if she'd somehow disappointed Matt in the lovemaking department.

He'd acted as if he had no alternative but to go to Houston, emphasizing that he'd made a commitment and that the client needed him. But Lauren didn't quite believe him. Perhaps what was most disturbing about it all was that she had realized she, too, was beginning to need him—especially when, with Matt, the client obviously came first.

LAUREN PULLED a brush from her cosmetic case and smoothed blusher onto her cheeks. The day of her mother's party had arrived and she was still husbandless. She'd talked to Matt by telephone several times and he'd told her he'd be back in time for the celebration. Still she couldn't help wondering what she would do if he didn't show. How could she explain his absence to her family and friends? What would they think of a bride being abandoned so soon after the wedding ceremony?

She stared at her reflection, poking her tongue out and examining it. "I wonder if I could say I'm too sick to come," she muttered. "No, it would never work. My folks would think me at death's door. I'm just going to have to face the music. Go with or without him. 'Marry in haste, repent in...'" Her voice trailed off. She went into the bedroom and glanced at the clock on the bedside table. They were due at the party in less than an hour.

With the tip of her pinkie, she smoothed some shadow onto her lids. The rat, she thought. If he didn't show up soon, she was going to call murder for hire.

Her silent tirade was interrupted by the telephone. "I'm back," Matt announced. "Is the party still on?"

Lauren felt like slamming down the receiver. No hello or how are you? No word of affection. No apologies for putting her through the agony of the past couple of hours. She wanted to tell him just what she thought of his inconsiderate treatment—but she couldn't. It wasn't part of the arrangement. She didn't have the right to get upset or angry. She was supposed to be independent. Not concerned with his business affairs. Agreeable all the time. Forget that, Lauren decided quickly, losing her temper. "Yes, the party's still on. Thanks for making me wonder all afternoon whether you were going to show up."

"Why would you worry about that? I wouldn't miss a party celebrating our marriage."

"Some marriage. Are you sure you're interested in continuing the arrangement?"

He was silent for what seemed like a full minute. "Are you trying to tell me something? Do you want out already?"

"Me want out? Maybe so, if your behavior the past week is any indication of the future."

"What behavior? Going on a business trip? I thought that was acceptable under our agreement." He chuckled. "You know what? I think you missed me. Don't worry. I'll make it up to you." He laughed again. "I'll be there in thirty minutes. Be ready to go." The receiver clicked in her ear.

Damn. Now what was she to do? She couldn't very well tell him to go jump in the lake. She needed him—at least tonight. She'd never live down the embarrassment if both of them didn't show up at her parents' party. But after the party, well, that was another matter altogether. "Missed me?" he'd bragged. The egotist! She'd had about enough of him and this makeshift marriage.

CHAPTER SIX

"WELL, ARE YOU READY?" He acted as if he was picking up a date—a not-too-satisfactory blind date, Lauren decided. Not so much as a peck on the cheek for his new bride as he appeared in the living room. His eyes took in her pink lace dress. "Nice dress," he commented offhandedly, then glanced at his watch. "We need to get going."

Lauren wished she had a cream pie handy to splat right in his face and cover up that smug expression. But she had a difficult time maintaining her anger. Matt looked so devastating, dressed in a trim black tuxedo—obviously custom-made. He must have gone by his apartment to dress. She stood like a statue for several moments, thinking surely he would cross the room and take her in his arms. Instead he merely glanced at his watch again. Lauren sullenly picked up her purse and walked ahead of him out the front door.

"A limousine?"

"I thought your parents would expect it." He signaled to the driver to remain inside and opened the door for Lauren himself.

Once they were in the car, Lauren reached up and closed the panel separating them from the driver.

"You want to be alone?" Matt had a poker face, except for his eyes. They were twinkling.

"Not necessarily. How was your trip?"

"I didn't think you'd be interested," Matt said. "I'm not used to providing my business partners with a play-by-play of my daily activities."

Lauren watched him from across the expanse of leather seat. He seemed to be enjoying this.

"I'll be happy to tell you all about it." He picked up her hand and nestled it between his own. "Naturally I'll expect the same in return, though. How did you spend your week?"

Lauren didn't want to report in, either, she realized. But that was foolish. She couldn't expect something from Matt that she was unwilling to give herself. Her answer was noncommittal. "Oh, the usual—work, play... you know."

Matt responded in kind. "Well," he said, "likewise for me."

And that was the extent of their conversation.

The limousine moved past the parked vehicles lining the drive of the country club and stopped at the front entrance. A uniformed attendant opened Lauren's door, but as she moved to get out, Matt stopped her. His arm went around her shoulder and his lips moved to hers. For a moment all was forgotten but the pressure of his mouth on hers. A discreet cough from the attendant brought her to her senses and she pushed away, feeling rather bereft when Matt moved back across the seat to open his door.

"Darlings!" Her mother was beaming as they walked through the double doors of the club. "We thought you'd never get here."

"Sorry, Mother. Matt got tied up with a client."

"Well, I'm just glad you're finally here." Her mother put herself between Matt and Lauren, and, linking arms, the three headed into the guest-filled room.

An hour later Lauren was leaning against the fireplace cornered by one of her father's commercial-account officers, Jack Something-or-other. He was young and handsome and had been one of the many men her parents had invited to their home primarily to meet Lauren. She had dated Jack once—it had taken only once to know he wasn't for her.

Jack had wanted a wife—a wife to take care of, to subjugate—a wife who'd have dinner on the table at six and who'd make sure his shirts got to the laundry, or better yet, iron them herself. He was simply one of any number of nice men whose goals were at odds with Lauren's. Men who had passed through her life and had been given little of her attention. And Jack wasn't getting her attention at the moment as he droned on about municipal bond funds. Instead her eyes and her mind were focused on a man across the room.

Matt was sequestered in a corner with a willowy brunette. A stranger to Lauren. Lauren kept fighting off stabs of annoyance at the number of women at the party who knew Matt. She was surprised at how many mutual acquaintances she and Matt had, especially since their paths had never crossed prior to her placing the ad. The brunette appeared to be more than a mere acquaintance, and Lauren was becoming more than a little annoyed. Matt had already danced with the woman twice, and now they were engrossed in conversation, her hand resting on his arm. Who was she? Had anyone else at the party noticed the amount of time the two had spent together? Lauren hoped not. How would it look if people figured out the groom had spent more time with this interloper than he had with his bride?

"Would you excuse me, Jack?" Lauren broke away from the conversation and started moving across the room. She knew she was acting like an insecure wife, but she couldn't help it. At first she was puzzled by her emotional reaction at seeing other women flirt with her husband—then it became all too clear. For the first time in her life, she was jealous. There was no use kidding herself, no use trying to convince herself this was only a business arrangement. So what if it'd started out like that? Somewhere along the way, she'd fallen in love.

Maybe she'd even loved Matt Kennerly from the very beginning—the emotions he could spark in her that nobody else ever had, the way she'd secretly looked forward to their few dates, though all the while protesting, the warm giddy feeling she had when she'd first seen him at their wedding. Lauren had tried to push the notion aside. It scared her to realize how much she cared, especially since she doubted Matt felt the same way, or for that matter, would ever feel the same way.

After all, what could he possibly need her for? A companion? Hardly. That woman across the room seemed perfectly willing to provide lots of companionship. Social standing—as the son-in-law of Lyle Grayson? Judging from the number of people he knew tonight, he needed no help in that department.

Again, that niggling thought crept into her brain. She tried to keep it from surfacing, but it was still there. Why had Matt married her? Could he possibly be as taken with her as she was with him? No. He certainly wasn't acting like a man in love. But there was no denying the chemistry between them. She'd felt it almost from the beginning, still felt it now. And she knew he did, too. So why had he cut short their honeymoon? His client might have needed him, but there had been no indication that it was for a life-or-death matter.

Lauren realized she was getting nowhere with her train of thought. There was just one thing to remember: while she might not be a success in winning Matt's love, she did have a legal document saying she was his wife. And by gosh, she wasn't about to be supplanted by another female. It was time for her to take her husband in hand. Literally.

"I was wondering when you'd get the fire in your eyes." Melissa stopped Lauren as she crossed the room. "What's with all these unattached predatory females? One was after Roger earlier."

"Who is she, anyway?" Lauren gestured with her head toward Matt and his companion. "There are so many strangers here we need name tags."

"Well, according to Dee, that brunette's tag would read Old Girlfriend. Now take it from a mature married woman—" her sister-in-law laughed "—get over there and break up that little tête-à-tête."

Matt moved away from the brunette as Lauren approached, and the woman's proprietary hand fell from his sleeve.

"I don't believe I've met your friend, darling." Lauren rested a hand on Matt's arm, mimicking the other woman's actions. "I'm Lauren Kennerly." She emphasized the word Kennerly.

"Suzanne Morgan," the woman said.

"So sorry to interrupt—" Lauren's voice was insincere "—but I must claim my husband for a dance. This is our song." She took Matt's hand and pulled him away.

"'Moonglow' is our song?"

Lauren shrugged. "It'll do until we get a real one."

They moved out to the patio where a buffet and a portable dance floor had been set up beside the pool. A gazebo doubled as a bandstand and a five-piece ensemble was playing.

Matt put his arm around her waist. "We've never danced together."

"We haven't, have we?" Lauren was surprised. "It seems that—" She stopped. She wasn't about to let Matt know how she felt.

"What were you going to say?"

"Nothing."

"Lauren, what did you start to say?"

"That we've hardly had a chance—you've been too busy dancing with every unattached female in sight to bother with your wife."

He laughed. He seemed to be laughing a lot tonight, Lauren thought. Well she was glad someone was enjoying this farce.

"I feel like that, too, sometimes."

"Like what?"

"Don't be obtuse, Lauren. Like there are a lot of things we haven't done. Is that what you started to say? Admit it." His look told her he already knew the answer.

Matt pressed his hand against Lauren's back and molded her body into his. They moved to the nostalgic tune as if they'd been dancing together forever. Lauren's arms were around his neck, her nostrils filled with the aroma of his after-shave, mingled with a scent that was distinctly Matt. She had to stifle a tremble, such was the effect the man was having on her senses. She wondered if she could be affecting him the same way. The thought gave Lauren an idea. She would use her womanly charm to make sure Matthew Kennerly was not immune to her, that he forgot all about his old girlfriends. She snuggled her body closer to his. A red-tipped fingernail wriggled beneath his collar and stroked his neck, as she placed a few light kisses on his ear. She could feel the increased pound of his heartbeat.

"Keep that up and this party's going to get damn interesting," he said.

Lauren moved her body even closer to Matt's.

"Lauren—" his voice sounded pained "—I'm not going to be able to leave the dance floor."

She laughed and eased away slightly, feeling a certain sense of power. She could make Matt want her. He might not love her, but he did desire her. For now, that would have to be enough. "Would you like to just slip away?"

He laughed. "I think escape's going to be impossible for a while." He nodded his head toward her father who was signaling for everyone to come back inside.

Lauren and Matt moved back inside through the French doors, appreciating the contrast of refrigerated air in the room to that of the humid summer night. Lyle Grayson was standing on the small dais, a microphone in his hand and Jeanette by his side. Roger, L.J., Melissa and Dee stood nearby.

"Friends, could I have your attention a few minutes? Princess, Matt, come on up here." They joined Lyle on the dais. Lyle motioned to the waiters holding trays with tulip-shaped glasses. "Let's get everyone some champagne." After the waiters had moved through the crowd, he held his own glass high. "To my daughter Lauren— who has excellent judgment—and to her husband, Matt, who likewise exhibits impeccable taste. Health, happiness—and a nice crop of Grayson grandchildren."

The crowd twittered good-naturedly and Lauren felt her face redden. Matt bent his head and murmured in her ear. "To Lauren, the best reason I've found yet to read the newspaper."

Lauren laughed, her tension easing for the first time in days. Maybe everything would work out after all.

"Do you think the guilty party's here tonight?" Matt's eyes scanned the people scattered around the room. "The anonymous matchmaker?"

"Could be," Lauren said, her eyes resting on Casey. She didn't think now was the time to tell Matt about Casey's confession.

He nuzzled her neck. "Well, I'm beginning to wonder if I don't owe the culprit a vote of thanks."

"Hey, you two lovebirds..." L.J. was speaking into the microphone. Lauren self-consciously pulled away from Matt, but his strong arms brought her back against his side. "Roger and I have come up with a little toast for the newlyweds. So pay attention." The brothers' voices rang out in unison:

"We said it could never be done,
Almost thirty and under the gun,
Then Lauren met Matt,
They clicked just like that
And decided that two could be one."

The guests began to groan. "Not Grayson limericks!" someone called out.

"Quiet," Roger chided. "We've only just begun. It gets better...and raunchier—"

"Boys!" Jeanette Grayson raised her hands up to her face in embarrassment.

"Sorry, Mother." L.J. wadded up the piece of paper. "To Matt and his new bride—we're glad he can afford a cook. It's a cinch he didn't marry one."

"Who cares whether she can cook." Matt laughed, placing a brief kiss on her lips, then another as Lauren moved her arms to encircle his neck. After a long kiss, he pulled away to the applause of their audience. Again Lauren tried to escape, to put a respectable distance between them, but Matt kept her close. For the first time Lauren had a feeling of contentment, as if their marriage was real. *It is real,* she reminded herself. *Maybe Matt and I entered into this arrangement quickly, but it wasn't frivolously. It wasn't. We both planned for the marriage to work—to work forever.*

His arm clamped firmly around her waist, Matt moved away from the crowd. "Do you think we might make a getaway pretty soon? I'm beat. I hadn't planned on spending this week working like a fiend, but that's what I've been doing. Oh, there's Wes. You should meet him before we go." Wes Fullerton and Matt were partners in a North Dallas real-estate project.

"Why don't you bring him over here? My feet are killing me." Lauren eased a foot out of one of her heels and wiggled her toes. "They're still smarting from all those times you stepped on them while we were dancing."

Matt's knuckles stroked her cheek. "That's your fault for distracting me." He smiled. "Be right back."

Casey tapped Lauren on the shoulder just as Matt stepped away and said:

"I admit I thought Lauren mad
When she resorted to placing an ad,
But now she whispers with glee,
'Don't you wish you were me'"

"Not you, too, Casey," Lauren interrupted, turning around to frown at her friend. "Have you been taking poetry-writing lessons from my brothers?"

"I rather enjoyed their little presentation—made me fully appreciate the term 'blushing bride.'"

"They embarrassed me to death. I'll be so glad to get this party over with and get on with my marriage and a normal routine."

"You sound smug. I suppose the ad wasn't such a bad idea after all. Even if I had to help it along a little. I think I'm going to try one myself—maybe you'll help me compose it."

"It's probably too soon to give a reading on whether it was a good idea." She smiled. "Remember George—and Rex."

"Still one terrific man out of three isn't bad. Speaking of terrific men—do you know that guy over by the bar?"

Lauren glanced over at a blond man in a white dinner jacket, then shook her head. "I've never seen him before. Probably somebody from Daddy's office."

"Then I'm sure he's overworked, lonely and needs someone to keep him company. Bye, Lauren."

Lauren sank down into a nearby chair to give her feet a rest while Matt, followed by Wes Fullerton, threaded his way back to her.

Matt had told her little about his plans for Phoenix Center, the project the two were developing, except that it would be a mixed-use complex.

"Wes, I want you to meet my wife, Lauren." Matt put his arm around her waist. "Lauren, Wes Fullerton."

Matt's business partner was a handsome man about the same age as Matt and half a head taller. "Your husband's a lucky guy," he said, shaking her hand. "What do you think about Phoenix Center, Lauren?"

"From the little I've heard it sounds wonderful. But I'd like to know more."

Wes smiled. "After meeting you, I'm beginning to understand why Matt's hardly given the project any of his attention the past couple of weeks. You'll have to come out and have a look at the site."

"I'd love to," she answered sincerely, instantly feeling comfortable with Wes.

"Great, anytime. Of course, there's going to be a lot more to see in a few weeks. Right now it's just a big hole in the ground." He patted Matt on the shoulder. "Congratulations again, old man. And good luck to you, Lauren. You're going to need it married to Mr. Intense here." Wes moved away in the direction of the bar.

Mr. Intense? Sure Matt worked hard, but Wes's comment still struck Lauren as a bit strange. She shrugged it off as Matt's whisper interrupted her thoughts. "When do you think we can get away?"

Lauren glanced at her watch. It was almost twelve-thirty. "If we wait until the guests leave, we won't get a bit of sleep tonight. And we both have to work tomorrow."

"I wasn't really thinking about sleep. But I would like to get to bed...."

A short time later, their chauffeur dropped them off, and Matt and Lauren walked to the front door of her house, arm in arm.

"That was the longest damned limo ride in history," Matt said as he fished in his pocket for his key. "I had half a mind to say to hell with propriety and claim my husbandly prerogatives right in the back seat."

Lauren giggled. "You wouldn't have."

"Oh, no? If I don't find this key soon, you'll see the degree of my impatience." He searched in his breast pocket.

"Here." Lauren handed him her key. "Open the door before you make a spectacle of yourself—and me—in front of the neighbors."

Matt stretched as they entered the foyer. "Mmm, it's great to be alone—finally. Come here, woman." He snapped her against him. "Now tell me how much you missed me."

"Were you gone? I hadn't noticed."

Matt pinned her arms down in a rough hug and whispered, "Tell me or I'll hug you to death."

"All right. I missed you a little. Now loosen your hold so I can breathe."

Matt relaxed his grip and his eyes locked with hers. His stare was as demanding in its intensity as his arms had been, the gray irises molten with desire.

Lauren felt a flush of longing as his lips moved toward hers, and she tilted her chin to receive his kiss. Her arms wrapped around his neck as his hands moved to her back to press her hard against his body. His fingers groped for her zipper and began undoing the back of her dress.

"Let's go upstairs," she whispered, her voice giving away her intense desire for Matt and his lovemaking. He took her hand, leading her up the staircase. She felt exhilarated knowing that even though Matt had deserted her on their honeymoon, it wasn't because of dissatisfaction with their sexual relationship. The knowledge was a small victory, but the heady feeling of satisfaction was fleeting. It was soon replaced by a more demanding, unmet hunger as she and Matt reached the landing and he reached for her from behind, gently pushing aside her hair and kissing her nape, as his hands traced the contours of her body. Then he turned her slightly and lifted her, carrying her into the bedroom.

LAUREN OPENED HER EYES and stretched languidly. The pillow beside her was empty; Matt was already up. She could smell coffee brewing.

When she walked into the kitchen Matt was sitting at the table reading the newspaper. He was dressed in a dark pin-striped suit and a pale yellow dress shirt.

"I didn't realize all the bonuses of having a husband." She poured a cup of the steaming brew. "Ah…no more instant." She kissed him on the cheek.

He wrapped an arm around her waist and pulled her onto his lap. He peeked down the front of her cotton kimono and smiled, noticing the absence of anything underneath. "Be dressed like this when I get home." He gently pushed her away and rose, pulling a blue-and-yellow striped tie from the back of the chair. He wrapped it around his neck, deftly securing the knot without the benefit of a mirror. "Gotta go. I've got a grueling day— and week—ahead. See you." He picked up his keys from the cabinet and left through the back door.

LAUREN SAT in her office sipping bitter coffee, unable to concentrate. Another week of marriage had passed, then another. Not exactly the kind of marriage she envisioned. Admittedly she had neglected to think through the day-to-day details of living with someone. Perhaps she'd been too busy concentrating on the kind of marriage she *didn't* want to focus on what she did want.

All she and Matt seemed to do was work and make love. Most evenings they were both out until eight or later, and when Matt came home, he usually brought work with him. They were beginning to settle in, but Lauren felt it was almost as though she'd taken on a roommate with bedroom privileges instead of a husband. Matt was meticulously neat, always picking up after himself, never leaving so much as a coffee cup in the sink for her to transfer to the dishwasher. Matt took care of himself. Lucky for her. But Lauren didn't feel lucky—instead she felt confused, dissatisfied, vaguely troubled.

She wondered whether Matt felt the same. They didn't see enough of each other for Lauren to find out. There'd been no mention of house-hunting since before their marriage. Matt apparently still had his apartment. He'd only moved a few things to her place. She decided the situation must change. It was time to renegotiate, or at least to clarify, their arrangement. She dialed his office.

"Lunch?" Matt was obviously surprised that Lauren was calling. "Sure, where shall we meet?"

"Anywhere we can talk."

They met at twelve in a small wine bar on McKinney Avenue. Lauren toyed with her glass of Chablis while Matt watched her. She felt tense, unsure. What was she going to say? *Out with it,* she chided. *Say something.*

"We haven't seen much of each other lately."

"No. We've both been pretty busy." Matt took a sip of his wine.

"How are you?"

"Okay. Was the purpose of lunch to inquire about the state of my health?"

"Not exactly."

"Well?"

"Matt, we haven't talked enough about what we expect of our marriage. Merely that our careers were important and that we wanted a home and family."

He nodded, but offered nothing in reply.

His reticence wasn't making it any easier for her. "Our lives seem to be pretty much the same as before," she stated.

"I didn't think you wanted your life to change."

"Perhaps I didn't. Then again, maybe I wasn't being very realistic."

"I think I understand where you're coming from, and I can't say I disagree with you." He glanced down at his watch. "But I'm afraid now isn't the time to discuss it. Can we put it on hold a couple of days?"

Lauren didn't like the impatient frown on his face. Obviously there was no point in her continuing. She pulled her napkin from her lap and folded it beside her plate. "Sure," she replied. "Shall we go?"

Another week passed and Matt hadn't brought up their discussion again. Lauren wondered if she should reintroduce the subject. He'd seemed distracted, almost depressed all week. Why hadn't he talked to her? Wasn't that what marriage was all about—someone to share one's thoughts with? Matt didn't seem particularly keen on sharing anything. She tried to question him, to probe past his polite facade. "Another difficult case?" she asked after dinner.

"No, I'm just tired."

"Maybe you need to take a few days off."

"I'm too busy for that," he said impatiently.

"Keep up this routine and you'll end up sick. Then you'll have to take time off work."

"I don't have to do a damn thing. Would you get off my back?"

Lauren stormed up the stairs and slammed the bedroom door. An hour later, a contrite Matt was lying beside her, generous with his kisses and his apologies. But the truce was temporary and the problem grew worse.

Matt's workdays grew longer. Instead of coming home at eight or nine he didn't show up until nine-thirty, ten, sometimes eleven. It did no good to wait up for him—he was too unpredictable. Lauren began to wonder if he was seeing another woman. She didn't really think so—they'd talked about their relationship being based on fidelity. But every time she asked what was bothering him, Matt would only cut her off smartly, using his evasive courtroom techniques.

Lauren knew she should probably leave it alone, let Matt work out his own problems, but she had grown up in a talk-it-out household and just couldn't stand waiting any longer for him to tell her what was on his mind. So she decided to wait up for him one night.

"Is it Phoenix Center?" she asked. "Is something wrong there?"

"What makes you think that?" He climbed into bed.

Lauren thought she detected a defensiveness in his voice. "You haven't mentioned it lately, that's all."

"Maybe because I don't particularly consider my work any of your business. I don't poke my nose in Classic Interiors, so why don't you reciprocate and stay out of my affairs?" He flicked off his light and turned his body away from her. "Our professional lives have nothing to do with our marriage—I thought that was part of our agreement."

"I'm sorry." Lauren couldn't keep her voice from quavering. "I thought we'd gone beyond that, that we'd agreed to share our lives. I'm sorry I got confused about the ground rules. I assure you I won't interfere again." By this time the tears were falling freely—tears of anger and sadness.

Matt moved across the bed in an instant. "Hey, babe, I'm sorry." He gently wiped away her tears with his hands. "I'm really sorry." His lips moved to her eyes and kissed away the remaining moisture. The gentle kisses became more insistent as his tongue tasted the warmth of her mouth, meeting hers in a feverish reunion. Their bodies were soon aflame, their passion soothing the wounds inflicted by the cross words.

CHAPTER SEVEN

LAUREN COULD SMELL the lingering aroma of bacon when she padded into the kitchen in her nightgown. Matt's car was missing from the drive, evidence that he had already gone, gone without even saying goodbye. Despite their fervid lovemaking of the night before, Lauren knew they still had a problem. Matt was troubled, something was wrong, something he wasn't telling her about. He had apologized for barking at her, but he hadn't shared the reason for his distress.

What was happening to their marriage? Their partnership? Lauren had hoped they could strengthen a relationship that had started on a rather shaky foundation, but instead of the foundation solidifying, it seemed to be crumbling. She and Matt had spent so little time together. How could they build a marriage the way they were going? Did Matt even want to? Lauren couldn't help wondering whether he was regretting their hasty marriage, feeling bound to her because of their agreement.

"GIVE IT A LITTLE TIME," Casey suggested. "All marriages go through a period of adjustment."

"It's more than that," Lauren said. "I think he wants out."

"How can that be?" Casey scowled. "The man's crazy about you. Those aren't 'wanting out' looks I've seen on his face. Those are 'want' looks."

"How would you know? You haven't been around him since my parents' party. *I've* barely been around him since my parents' party." Her friend's words were soothing but did little to relieve her distress.

"The feelings behind the looks he gave you then and at the wedding don't fade. Now forget those insecure notions and hurry on out and get us a big fat contract. Decorating that new bank's gonna put money in our coffers."

"You mean it will if they sign. We've got some stiff competition on this one." Lauren stuffed a folder into her briefcase and put a couple of business cards into the pocket of her suit. "It's the largest project we've bid on yet."

"We can do it. Have faith." Casey closed the clasps on Lauren's briefcase, picked it up and passed it to Lauren. "Have faith in your marriage, too."

The interview with the vice-president of Century Bank went well, and Classic Interiors now had a freshly-signed contract for their biggest project ever. Still, the feeling of elation that Lauren usually experienced at getting a new customer, especially one this important, wasn't there. She was having difficulty thinking of anything except Matt.

As Lauren headed back down Dallas Parkway, she realized she wasn't ready to return to the office just yet. She was only a hop, skip and jump from the Phoenix Center site. Maybe she should stop by, and if Matt happened to be there, they could have lunch together.... She felt suddenly tense. Would Matt, reluctant as he had been lately about discussing the project, think she was butting into his business, perhaps even think she was spying on him? Lauren decided to take her chances and she turned into the construction site. She felt a strange mixture of relief and disappointment that Matt's coupe was nowhere around.

She got out of her car and peered through the chain-link fence surrounding the property. Wes was right—the site was basically just a big hole in the ground being made bigger and deeper by men operating heavy equipment. A large sign with a painting of the proposed complex stood at one corner of the lot, and Lauren walked over to have a look at it. Matt had showed her a sketch, but now she was able to imagine it finished on the lot.

"Lauren! What a surprise." Wes Fullerton came down the steps of the office trailer. His jacket was slung over one shoulder and his sleeves were rolled to the elbow. He slipped on sunglasses to ward off the bright sun. "Let me show you around."

"No need," Lauren replied. "I was just in the neighborhood and decided to take a quick peek."

"Well, what do you think?"

Lauren shrugged. In truth, it didn't look like much yet. But obviously that wouldn't be the most tactful thing to say to the enthusiastic Wes. "It's big." That was always a safe remark to make to a Texas businessman.

"Isn't it?" Wes beamed. "Why don't you come into the office and let me show you a scale model. And also offer you a cup of coffee. I've got a fresh pot brewing."

"That sounds great." As she climbed the stairs, Wes's hand rested on her back, lingering there a moment after they were inside. Lauren moved away. The small trailer seemed a little too cozy and intimate.

"Oh, it's beautiful." She studied the replica—the tall glass tower, the rounded roof, the terraced courtyard.

"Cream or sugar? Or do you prefer it black?"

"Black is fine." Lauren took the coffee from Wes. "Thank you."

"Anything for a lovely lady like you. You look especially gorgeous today."

"Thank you again," she said. This was the third time she'd seen Wes, and each time he had complimented her. Now he seemed to be studying her, and it made Lauren uncomfortable.

"It's after eleven," Wes said. "How about a bite of lunch?"

"I don't think so. I should get back to the office."

"You've got to eat lunch."

"Actually I generally don't," she fibbed. "Sometimes a carton of yogurt—but not much else. Helps me keep the extra pounds off."

"Well, it must work. You don't have any extra weight—except in the right places, of course," he said, looking her over. "We wouldn't want to spoil that perfect figure. Matt's a damn lucky guy. A wife with money and looks, too." His eyes again surveyed her body. "My condo's a mile or so away. I've got plenty of yogurt in the fridge. We could probably even rustle up a bottle of wine."

"Thanks, but I don't think so. I really have to be going." Lauren put down her coffee cup, picked up her handbag and moved toward the door.

Wes blocked her path. "Matt's been spending a lot of time at the office, a lot of evenings. Is there something wrong—something I could help with? I can be a good listener."

"Don't you think you're getting a little too personal?"

"Hey. I'm Matt's partner—just trying to be a pal. But I sure wouldn't ignore a little fortune cookie like you waiting at home." He put his hand on her arm.

Lauren glared at the unwelcome touch and Wes moved his hand. "Would you please step aside so I can get out of here?"

"Ah, come on. I don't see what the big rush is." Wes's smile became a leer. "After all, doll, you're the one who came by here."

"Get out of my way, you—"

"Now, now." He laughed, letting her pass. "Matt wouldn't like his wife saying naughty words, would he? I'll tell him you stopped by."

Lauren drove back to the office, perturbed about her run-in with Wes. She wondered what he'd tell Matt and what Matt would think. Surely he wouldn't believe that she was coming on to his business partner. But would he believe her if she told him Wes was putting the make on her? Lauren had no answers. Somehow she doubted if Matt would even be willing to discuss the situation. He didn't seem to want to talk about anything lately. And there was always the possibility he might blame her. A possibility she didn't want to risk right now.

Thoughts of Wes were forgotten when Lauren returned to her office. There were flowers from Matt on her desk—long-stemmed yellow roses—and two messages to call him. She dialed his number.

"Congratulate your husband on his self-restraint," he murmured.

"I'm afraid I don't understand."

"It took a lot of willpower to keep from waking you this morning...your hair was streaming provocatively across your cheek, the sheet had slipped down past your waist exposing all that creamy skin. You're a very desirable woman, Lauren. I think I'd like to have dinner with you tonight. Are you available?"

Lauren's head nodded in acquiescence, even though Matt could not see her. "Dinner...yes. Where?"

"Any place you like...or we could stay home and eat, or not eat..."

"I like the last suggestion," Lauren said. "But I think we'll need a little sustenance."

Matt chuckled. "I'll pick up something fast for dinner. You just come home early, okay?"

MATT CAME IN THE BACK DOOR, his arms filled with two grocery bags.

"Can I help?"

"Maybe unload these while I change," he answered, setting the bags on the kitchen counter. "It's hot as Hades out there."

He took off his suit jacket and loosened his tie. "Hello, babe." His voice was a gruff whisper.

"Hello," Lauren answered, smiling, her tension easing a little. It didn't appear Matt had spoken to Wes—he didn't act as though he knew about her visit to Phoenix Center.

Matt took her face in his hands. For a moment he just looked into her eyes, deeply, almost as though searching for her soul. His head moved to hers and their lips met, tentatively at first, then with more certainty. Lauren's arms moved up and around his shoulders, her fingers playing with the hair at the nape of his neck.

After a long moment, he released her. "I need a shower. I won't be long. Unless you want to help me?" He gave her a sly smile.

"I thought you were going to feed me," she said in a mock whine.

"A man's work is never done. I suppose I have to start the fire before I do anything else." He pulled a bag of charcoal from the storage cupboard and took it to the patio. Within minutes a flame darted into the air from the black-bowled grill. "I'll bet you want me to make you a drink, too." His mood was playful, a far cry from the one he'd been in lately.

"No, this is an equal-opportunity household, so I'll make the drinks. I'll even bring yours to you." She laughed. "Don't look so hopeful. I mean when you've finished in the shower."

"MAKING LOVE WITH YOU is wonderful." Matt's hands were tracing patterns across Lauren's collarbone. His gray eyes were silvery with passion. "I never want it to end."

"I feel the same way," Lauren responded, her own hands moving over Matt's body in a gentle exploration. The night had been a time of gentle courting, of romance. It was as though the happy-ever-after relationship Lauren had envisioned might really be possible. Ridiculous, Lauren reminded herself, her thoughts returning to Matt's behavior since their marriage. This was just a temporary interlude. What would tomorrow be like? Don't worry about that, she admonished herself. This spell was too precious to break. She smiled as Matt pulled her close to him. "Again . . . ?"

LAUREN DROVE to the office the following afternoon feeling relaxed—and it wasn't just because of the two margaritas. She'd just had a marvelous lunch with Matt and felt that everything was going to be fine. She'd taken the opportunity to confess her visit to Phoenix Center— although she didn't mention Wes—and hesitantly asked about its progress.

"Don't worry so much, Lauren," he'd said. "I know it doesn't look like much now. But it will come together. Besides, we've always got each other. Life's on an up-swing." After his reassurance, she'd even been able to put Wes Fullerton out of her mind.

"Marriage just takes some adjustment," she said aloud, her eyes on the traffic ahead of her. She knew she'd had to make some compromises. Well, obviously, so had Matt. Maybe it had just been more difficult for him than for her. What with all his responsibilities to his clients, and the extra work with Phoenix Center, his days must have been even more demanding and often un-pleasant. No wonder he didn't want to talk when he got home.

Her job was a lot less stressful than his, she rational-ized, at least most of the time. She'd have to take that into consideration from now on. Lauren was so deep in thought, she picked up only the tail end of a newscast mentioning Phoenix Center as she stopped for a red light. She quickly pushed a button to change the setting, hop-ing to catch more of the story on another station. "The bankruptcy of Wes Fullerton casts a long shadow over the future of the multi-faceted project. The question is whether his partner, Matthew Kennerly, can pull a rab-bit out of the hat and save the day as he does so often in the courtroom. Or will father-in-law, financier Lyle Grayson, have to come to the rescue?"

Cars honking broke Lauren's stupor as she realized the light had changed to green and she resumed her drive to-ward the office. She pulled into the parking lot and turned off the engine, remaining in the car for a few mo-ments, still stunned by the newscast. What had hap-pened? Should she call Matt? Would there be anything in the newspapers yet? She got out of the car and went into the office. The door was locked and she pulled out her key to let herself in. It was after three. Emily was already gone for the day and apparently Casey was out on a call.

Lauren walked over to the answering machine and played back the messages. One of the calls was from Matt saying he'd be back in touch. She phoned his office but got no further than the secretary. "I'm sorry, Mrs. Kennerly, but Mr. Kennerly is out for the rest of the afternoon."

The radio broadcast had left her with a sinking feeling. Why hadn't Matt told her there was a problem? Surely he must have known Wes was in trouble—more than likely that accounted for his recent foul mood. What had happened to break that mood? The night before and today at lunch Matt had acted as though he hadn't a care in the world. What was going on? Lauren knew only one thing—she had to find Matt and get some answers to her questions—soon.

She waited at the office for more than an hour hoping to hear from Matt. She tried to work, pulling out drapery samples and attempting to concentrate on window treatments, but it was hopeless—her brain just wouldn't focus on anything but the developments of the afternoon.

Lauren fixated on the telephone, willing it to ring, but the obstinate bell remained silent. She even picked up the receiver once to make sure it was working and placed it back in the cradle when she heard the dial tone. When another half hour had passed, she was tired of waiting and decided to lock up for the day. Maybe she could get home in time to catch the early news.

Just as she'd closed the office door, Lauren heard the peal of the telephone. She'd forgotten to turn on the answering machine, and she searched through her keys, fumbling in her haste to find the right one, then dropped the entire ring onto the sidewalk. Finally she got the door unlocked and pushed it open, only to have the ringing stop the moment she stepped inside. Had the caller been Matt? she wondered, totally frustrated and hesitating for a few moments to see if the phone would ring again. But no luck. Dejectedly she switched on the machine and walked out the door to her car.

Lauren arrived home and parked the car in the front, not bothering to pull it into the garage. She picked up the evening newspaper lying in the grass, unfolding it as she headed up the walk. There was nothing on the front page about Phoenix Center, nothing in the business section, either.

She kicked off her beige pumps as she entered the hall, then passed through to the kitchen to be greeted by Pandora, purring and rubbing against her leg. "Okay, I know you're hungry," she said, bending down to pull a bag of cat food out from under the counter. She poured an ample supply of the dry mixture into a bowl.

Now that the cat was satisfied, Lauren leaned on the counter to scan the rest of the newspaper. Not a thing. Apparently Wes's bankruptcy filing had come too late for the afternoon deadline. She left the paper on the counter and went into the living room to switch on the television. But it wasn't yet five—too early for the news.

Lauren went upstairs to her bedroom and changed into a pair of white shorts and a blue-and-green striped T-shirt, then came back downstairs to plop in front of the television screen, Pandora filling her lap, when the news began. "A prominent Dallas businessman goes bust," intoned the newscaster. "That and more news in a moment."

"Has the golden corridor turned to brass? Local entrepreneur Wes Fullerton shocked the business community today by filing for bankruptcy. This puts a big question mark on the status of Phoenix Center, his latest multi-million dollar project. For more details, here's Angela Benson on the scene at Phoenix Center."

"This is Angela Benson, and behind me is the Phoenix Center Project, the dream of Wes Fullerton and his business partner, Matthew Kennerly. Today that dream may have turned into a financial nightmare. Here's Mr. Kennerly now. Let's see if we can get a word with him."

Matt's image appeared on the television screen as he attempted to brush past the gathering of media people. When the commentator pushed against his arm and thrust the microphone in front of his face, Matt assumed his commanding courtroom glower—the same glower he'd given Lauren the day they'd met. "Sorry, but I have no comment at this time." A grim-looking Matt moved away from the crowd and into the office trailer.

Lauren wished her terrible anxiety would ease. She didn't like what was going on in her brain; she was starting to feel panicky. Something was out of place—a jigsaw puzzle with a piece missing. Why hadn't Matt told her about the problems with Phoenix Center? Why had he been the attentive, adoring husband last night and earlier today with this disaster pending? She thought back to their first meeting—Matt disagreeable and distant. Then, all of a sudden, within a matter of hours, he'd begun to pursue her like a child chasing an ice-cream truck on a summer afternoon. Of course, by then he had discovered she was Lyle Grayson's daughter. Was there a connection between her family fortune and her desirability? Did Matt know from the start that these financial problems were imminent?

The announcer's comments from the earlier radio report still irked Lauren—especially the part about her father and his possible financial backing. And, she recalled, Wes, too, had mentioned the Grayson money. Her social standing had been an issue with men before—but not of late. Over the years Lauren had encountered more than a few fortune hunters, men who were more impressed with the family's money than with her personal appeal. But not Matt. She had ruled him out as a guy with dollar signs in his eyes. Had she been wrong?

Lauren didn't want to believe the ugly thoughts now playing through her mind. She tried to push them away. If only Matt would get in touch with her.

Lauren stared at the telephone. The broadcast had been live. That meant Matt was in the trailer—with a telephone handy. "Call," she demanded, and as though in response, her phone rang.

"Hello, Matt? Oh...Dee, how are you feeling? Yes, I've seen the news. No, I don't know anything yet. I'm trying to keep the line open in case Matt calls. Yes, I'll try not to worry. Thanks for caring." Lauren hung up.

She had just settled back in her chair when the doorbell chimed. She hurried to answer it, thinking it might be Matt without his key, even though it was unlikely he could make it home that quickly. She tried to hide her disappointment when she opened the door to Jeanette Grayson.

"Darling—" Jeanette hugged her daughter as she came into the hall "—I heard the news on the car radio and since I was only a few blocks away, I just took a chance on your being here. Have you heard from Matt?"

Lauren shook her head.

"Well, don't you worry. I'm sure he's terribly busy right now, what with the publicity and all. Listen, I can't stay. I've got to run. Your father went to Austin yesterday and I'm on my way to pick him up at the airport. But I wanted to tell you we're here for you and Matt. Of course you know that." She patted Lauren's cheek. "Daddy will be behind Matt all the way—no matter what it takes. If it's money he needs—"

"Thanks, Mother," she interrupted. "Maybe that won't be necessary."

"I hope not," Jeanette answered. "But if it is, all Matt has to do is ask. After all, he's family now." She looked at her watch. "I've got to dash. You know how impatient your father is when he has to wait. I don't know why he refuses to take taxis."

The six-o'clock news was a repeat of the news at five, except for the addition of a shot of Matt leaving the Phoenix Center site. He still hadn't telephoned home, a fact that disturbed Lauren no less than her mother's visit. As well-intentioned as it might have been, Jeanette's message hadn't comforted Lauren at all, but simply called to the surface doubts Lauren had been trying to repress ever since the night Matt had talked her into a hasty wedding. Now those doubts were rearing up and hitting right in the pit of her stomach. As far as her marriage was concerned, this was a serious blow, a blow that might be fatal. For the first time in weeks, she felt she had her eyes wide open. Lauren feared she finally knew the real reason Matt had married her.

She spent the next few hours alternately trying to concentrate on the television set and pacing the den like a caged lioness. Three times the telephone rang, and each time she raced to it as if it were her lifeline. One call was from Casey, another from a carpet-cleaning company and the last from a marketing-research pollster. Nothing from Matt. Finally exhaustion took its toll and Lauren collapsed onto the couch, Pandora curled at her feet. She had dozed off when she heard a car door slam. She sat up as Matt came into the room.

"Hi, babe." He bent to kiss her cheek, then leaned over to stroke the cat, but it ran through his legs and darted outside. "That damn animal—just what I need when I've had such a rotten day."

Lauren padded to the door, retrieved Pandora and came back in with the pet in her arms. "I wouldn't know anything about your day. Not from you, that is. All I know is what I read in the paper or hear on the news. It certainly isn't from anything my husband told me."

"Looks like I've stumbled into a beehive." The warmth was gone from Matt's voice. "Apparently I've got one more problem than I realized." He walked over to the bar, Lauren trailing behind, and poured himself a Scotch on the rocks. "Okay, out with it. You're upset because I didn't call. Right?"

"That's part of it—why didn't you call me? Why did I have to learn about the bankruptcy of my husband's partner from the radio?"

"I did try to call once. But obviously I've been busy— you can't imagine how busy." Matt took a swallow of the Scotch and grimaced. "I tried to get hold of you as soon as I heard about Wes, but I couldn't reach you. I guess you hadn't had time to get back to the office. I wasn't able to call again. I thought you'd understand."

"So why didn't you tell me yesterday or the day before that Wes was going to declare bankruptcy?"

Matt sighed. "Because I didn't know it myself until today. In case you haven't heard, businessmen don't announce to the world they're about to go belly up. They just drop the bomb and let the chips fall where they may. Sometimes they don't even tell their own partners. I knew there was trouble, but I didn't realize it was this bad. I thought I could handle it." He drained his glass.

"So you knew there was trouble and you didn't tell me. Why?"

"Maybe I wanted to protect you—to keep you from worrying."

"Keep the little woman in the dark, don't you mean? I'm not some child who needs to be insulated from the real world, and you know it. Why didn't you prepare me for this?"

"Why, why, why! What is this? Twenty Questions?"

"Excuse me for being interested in my own husband's well-being. I thought our marriage allowed for some wifely concern."

"I was just trying to spare you the anxiety." Matt patted her on the shoulder, but Lauren pulled away.

"Is that the real reason, or was there some other motive?"

"And what would that be? I don't know what's wrong with you tonight. All these questions and petty complaints."

"I'm sorry to bother you with my petty complaints. I guess I should just shut up and start writing checks."

"What the hell do you mean by that?" Matt's eyes had turned into thunderclouds.

"It seems all I seem to be good for is petty complaints and petty cash—only the Grayson cash isn't so petty, is it? How much money do you need for Phoenix Center?"

"You seem to have everything figured out, don't you?" He moved to the bar, unscrewed the top from the bottle of Scotch and filled his glass again. "What makes you think your appeal is limited to your financial assets?" He crudely surveyed her body. "You're good for one other thing, at least."

Lauren's eyes narrowed. "So you got a few unexpected fringe benefits. Why should you feel any compunction about using me physically—as well as financially?"

"You enjoyed it as much as I did. Don't deny it."

"Why should I deny it—you're okay in bed yourself—but that's not the issue."

"Ah, yes, that damn Grayson money is the issue. I didn't realize you harbored such thoughts in your little mind, Lauren." There was a strong emphasis on little.

"Look me in the eye and tell me my father has no part in Phoenix Center."

"Like hell I will."

"Ha, I knew it. I knew you got to him through me. My vision is a lot clearer than it was a few weeks ago."

"Mine, too—definitely twenty-twenty tonight. Thanks for the vote of wifely confidence."

His words stung. Lauren had really wanted a denial, an explanation, an interpretation of what had happened that day, other than the one that was unfolding. Instead, Matt was standing there trading insults with her and refusing to deal with her concerns. His non-denial was a tacit admission that she was right, that he'd married her for the money, that their marriage really was a business arrangement. A very one-sided one. Lauren felt rage and hurt build up within her. "Get out! I want you out of my house—out of my life."

"No way. I'm staying right here." Matt gave her a smile that resembled a sneer. "If we split up now, the timing would ruin me. Like you said, I need the tie to your family to get out of this bind. You made a deal and you're going to stick with it. Like me, you'll live up to your side of the bargain. I think even you will admit I've been keeping my part of this agreement." His eyes again surveyed her body.

What gall! Did he think entertaining her in bed fulfilled his side of the agreement? What did that make him then—some sort of gigolo? Her money in exchange for his favors?

Lauren bit the inside of her cheek to keep from bursting into tears. Her doubts, her worst fears were being confirmed. That was all their marriage had ever been to Matt—a business agreement. "You're despicable," she hissed.

"No. I'm realistic. You just can't handle it spelled out like that. We made a deal—a bargain—and damn it, you'll stand by your word. I need you now."

"And when you no longer need me..."

"When that day comes, we'll be through." Matt's face was hard, his jaw clenched. "I certainly don't need this kind of wifely devotion. I work every day with bad marriages—I don't care to live one, too."

"So you plan to stay until you're good and ready to get out."

"You got it."

"Any other dictates?"

"Yes. No one is to know about this little scene tonight or that there is anything amiss in our relationship. *No one.*"

Lauren glared at him through narrowed eyes. She wanted to rush at him and hit him in frustration. But she wasn't going to give him the satisfaction of seeing her succumb to hysteria. She took a deep breath. "Well, it looks like you have me just where you want me," she said coolly. "I certainly can't throw you out bodily, and I have no intention of calling the police and embarrassing myself and my family further. So stay. But don't plan on enjoying yourself.''

"We'll see about that." He moved toward her.

"What are you doing?"

"What does it look like?"

Lauren could smell the whiskey on his breath, and in his eyes she thought she saw the same frustration she was feeling. For a fleeting second she wondered if he might strike her. "Damn you, Lauren," he cursed just before his lips crushed hers and his arms pulled her against his hard body.

She tried to pull away, to resist the force of his lovemaking. She didn't want to be his lover any longer, yet her initial reluctance faded under Matt's experienced caresses. She despised the weakness that turned her rage into hot desire. He carried her into the bedroom. She could almost hear herself gasping, begging for that final ecstasy. And, as always, she climbed that heavenly spiral... Her body arched to Matt's in a final release. Then, too soon, he moved away from her. He lay still on the far side of the king-sized bed, several feet separating them. Lauren felt used as she got up from the bed and headed for the shower.

She picked up the bar of soap and gently lathered her body, leaning back under the hot stream of water to rinse away the sudsy residue. She was exhausted—but, more than that, utterly frustrated. What was she going to do? Matt had warned her to tell no one about their problems. Their life was to appear to go on as before.

But how could she keep up this charade when everything had changed? Her disappointment in Matt went to the very core of her being. Unfortunately all the negative thoughts did not obliterate the love she still felt for him—that was something that would never change.

Suddenly she realized how blessedly simple her life had been before she'd met Matt. All that time she'd wasted worrying about becoming thirty and never having fallen in love. Love wasn't an emotion she'd wish on her worst enemy. Love was an aching pain that hurt more than she'd have believed possible, yet, ironically, she couldn't imagine a life without Matt....

When she returned to the bedroom, Matt was gone. He didn't return home that night. Lauren went to bed at one, but tossed and turned for hours, finally falling into an exhausted sleep around four. When she awoke at seven she felt just as miserable as the night before. Could she have misjudged Matt? she wondered. No, he had as good as admitted she was right. Despite that, she regretted not giving him a chance to tell his side of the story. She wished he would talk to her—really talk to her and explain himself. She deserved that. But would it be possible after all their angry words? Maybe she'd try to call him later in the morning. If they were going to live together, they couldn't exist in total silence. Or at least Lauren couldn't. It was against her nature.

But apparently her husband had no such problem. Lauren tried his office at ten. Matt was out. She left a message for him to return her call. When she hadn't heard from him by three, she called again. This time his secretary apologized, "Mr. Kennerly is unable to come to the phone right now." Lauren finally reached Matt at six that evening.

"Are you coming home?"

"To what do I owe this touching concern?" Matt's voice was cold.

"I think we need to talk."

"I've been talking all day. I have no interest in further conversation."

"Have it your way," she sighed. "But are you coming home?"

"Expect me when you see me." Then he hung up.

At eleven o'clock that night Lauren heard Matt's car pull into the drive. She was already in bed, all the lights out. Should she get up? No, she decided. It was better just to stay put—heaven knew she was in no shape for a confrontation. She lay still, listening to Matt puttering about, his greeting to Pandora—"Hello, you overweight feline"—the opening and closing of the refrigerator, the sound of a late-night talk show.

About an hour later Matt came into the bedroom. He left the lights off, but she could make out the silhouette of his body. He removed his tie and hung it over the doorknob, next came his shirt, which he draped over a chair. She saw his hands go to the buckle of his belt and heard the rasp of the zipper being pulled downward. Soon he was nude, his muscular body gleaming in the darkness.

When he climbed between the cool cotton sheets, she could smell the mint of toothpaste and the faint aroma of his after-shave. For an instant, Lauren wanted to reach for him, to comfort him, to comfort herself. But she was afraid she would only be rebuffed. The bed moved as Matt turned his back to her. She soon heard the soft breathing of a sound slumber. But sleep again eluded her until the early hours of morning.

"You look awful." Casey wasn't one to beat around the bush.

"Thanks a lot." Lauren threw her briefcase onto the yellow Queen Anne chair in the reception area. "That's just what I needed to hear."

"I'm sorry. I didn't mean to be so blunt. But you do. There are bags under your eyes and your skin's as white as a ghost's. Lauren, you're making yourself sick worrying about this mess with Wes Fullerton. Is Matt real upset?"

"I'm not sure. He's working so many late hours I haven't got to talk to him much," Lauren hedged.

"Well, how do *you* feel?"

"Miserable. But it's probably as much the dog days of summer as anything." She fanned herself with a copy of *Metropolitan Home*.

"Six days of one-hundred-degree-plus temperatures. And there's not a break in sight, according to the weatherman. Good old Dallas in August. Are you positive, though, it isn't something else?"

"What else could it be?" Lauren asked.

"Well—" Casey eyed her up and down "—you could be in a family way. Are you?"

"Isn't that a rather personal question?"

"Since when have I avoided being personal with you? So? Are you?"

"No, Miss Busybody. The only expectant mothers in my family are Melissa and Dee, and they're both about a week overdue."

"Okay, just checking." Her blue eyes looked troubled as she stared at Lauren. "What's really wrong? And don't say nothing, because we've known each other too long for that."

"This Phoenix Center thing has just put a lot of stress on us. That's all. I'm not sleeping too well."

"Why don't you go back home then? Maybe you could catch a couple of hours sleep now."

"Thanks, but I have to dash out to the Century Bank. I've got some new ideas I want to run by their staff before we place an order for the materials. Maybe I'll go on home from there, though, if you don't mind.''

"I don't mind, I insist.''

Lauren purposely avoided the Parkway on her way home from the bank. She didn't want to go near the Phoenix Center area—there were enough bad images in her brain as it was. But the circuitous route she took really didn't help. She might be able to put the center out of sight, but unfortunately she couldn't get it out of mind.

Why was she allowing one incident to dominate her entire existence? Because Matt had taken over all her thought processes, that was why. She couldn't seem to concentrate on anything except her husband. Would Matt be home tonight? Would anything be different if he were?

"This is ridiculous,'' Lauren scolded herself. "You never dreamed you'd end up one of those women who paces the floor wondering if her husband will show. Are you just going to be a doormat and hang around waiting for him? Heck no.'' Impulsively she pulled up to a convenience store, got out of her car and headed for the pay telephone.

"Casey? Matt's going to be late tonight. How about catching a movie and having a bite to eat? Maybe even do a little shopping?''

LAUREN ARRIVED HOME about one in the morning. Her feistiness had deserted her, and she was feeling decidedly guilty. She'd tried to convince herself all the way home that she had nothing to be guilty about. If Matt didn't feel the need to account for his whereabouts, then why should she? Sauce for the gander and all that. Still, the feelings wouldn't go away.

The house was dark when she drove up, but Matt was home—his car was in the garage. She entered stealthily on tiptoe, hoping to catch him unaware, but her attempt at quiet was foiled by the cat meowing a raucous hello. She shushed Pandora and moved upstairs to the bedroom. The lights were out and Matt was in bed, either asleep or pretending to be.

Somehow this irritated Lauren. After dragging poor tired Casey all over Northpark and the Greenville strip, and being dead on her feet herself, Lauren felt she deserved some kind of attention regarding her late arrival. She wanted to turn on the lights, the bedroom television, make all sorts of noise. She even considered setting off the security alarm. She was spoiling for a confrontation, a chance to ventilate.

But Lauren knew that wasn't going to happen. At least not yet. Obviously Matt had made a decision not to acknowledge her tardiness, just as she had let his lateness the night before seemingly go unnoticed. This was not going to be the time for battle. It would eventually come, of that Lauren was certain. There was just too much tension between them for a peaceful coexistence to continue indefinitely.

CHAPTER EIGHT

"GOOD MORNING." Matt was standing against the door frame, a cup of coffee in his hand. He was dressed for work. "There's coffee made. You could probably use some."

She didn't answer. Was he trying to take her to task for her late night? Well, tough. And if he wanted to know where she'd been, he would have to ask. Lauren would tell him exactly how she'd spent the evening before. She had no secrets. But she wasn't going to volunteer an explanation any more than he ever had.

"Anything you want to say before I leave?" The tone of Matt's voice told her he wanted her to say more.

"Not really."

"Have it your way." He picked up his keys from a tray on top of the chest of drawers and put them in his trouser pocket.

Matt's cool demeanor annoyed Lauren. She threw the sheet back and got up. Her sheer nightgown, which had twisted around her during the night righted itself and draped clingingly to her body as she walked. She was halfway across the room when she noticed Matt watching her. He had let down his guard for an instant and she could see the desire in his eyes. But when their eyes met, the veil of self-control fell back over his face, and he turned and left the room.

Lauren felt a sense of victory as she realized Matt still wanted her. Then the feeling vanished. So what if he did?

He'd made no secret of his physical cravings—but lust wouldn't change anything because lust didn't translate into love—and, despite everything, love was what she needed from him.

Lauren looked into the bathroom mirror and saw a wistful expression staring back. It didn't really matter what she needed. Their marriage, their life together, seemed to have a termination date on it and when that day came, it was bye-bye Matt. No use longing for something that was not meant to be. She pulled the gown over her head and stepped into the tub.

THE TIME HAD COME for Lauren to put her problems aside. She'd received a telephone call from both her brothers just before she left home. She was an aunt—twice.

A downpour threatened as she stepped out of her car in the parking lot at the hospital. She grabbed two stuffed animals, gifts for the babies, and held them close as she raced toward the entrance. She had just made it inside when a giant bolt of lightning split the sky to the north and big raindrops pelted the sidewalk.

It had been the usual hot, dry summer in Dallas. Lawns were turning brown and roses had stopped blooming. Only the durable crepe myrtles, with their blossoms of pink and white and lavender, brightened the parched landscape. The rain was much needed. But why did it have to start today when her spirits were at their lowest? As though to add insult to injury, she'd also left home without an umbrella. Oh well, maybe the shower would be over by the time she came back out. She had to be optimistic about something.

She clutched the two stuffed animals and made her way to the elevators leading to the maternity floor. Dee had delivered shortly before midnight and Melissa at four that morning—a baby girl apiece. Lauren had purchased two identical white teddy bears on the way to the hospital. She had been tempted to buy a third—they were so cuddly and irresistible. But then she got hold of her senses and remembered there was no baby in her future. No baby, no husband, no future.

Lauren pulled a tissue from her purse and dabbed at a tear rolling down her cheek. She was glad no one had witnessed this lapse into self-pity. She pulled a compact from her purse and patted her nose and cheeks with powder. She hoped her family wouldn't notice her red-rimmed eyes.

She got off the elevator and headed straight for the nursery. There they were, side by side—two pink-faced baby Grayson girls wrapped in pink blankets. The babies were incredibly cute, and Lauren felt a new pang, a new wave of sadness to add to her storehouse of misery.

Reluctantly she left the nursery window and moved down the hall to the room her sisters-in-law shared. The door was open and Lauren walked in. "Lauren," Dee said, on spying her. "Lauren," Melissa echoed, "have you seen our gorgeous daughters?"

Lauren moved between the beds and gave each of them a hug. "They are so darling. I don't know of two cuter little ones in the world."

"Just what a new aunt is supposed to say," Dee replied.

Lauren looked around the room. "The flowers are lovely." The area was filled with so many floral arrangements and plants that they covered all the available tables and windowsill space. A few had been placed on the floor against the wall.

"The pink roses are from Matt," Melissa said. "Wasn't that sweet?" She looked at Lauren. "Or was that your suggestion?"

Lauren looked up, surprised. "No, Matt didn't tell me he was planning to send flowers. I haven't even told him about the babies. He was already gone when I got the call."

"Roger and L.J. probably talked to him," Melissa said. "You must be so proud of Matt. He's the sweetest man, and he really seems to be turning this Phoenix Center thing around."

"Yes," Lauren mumbled. What did Melissa mean about Phoenix Center? She couldn't very well ask for explanations. A wife should know about her husband's activities. "Oh," she said, "I forgot about these." She handed each of the women one of the white stuffed animals.

"I wondered if you were going to part with them," Dee said, "the way you were holding on. But thanks. Sarah and Amanda will love them."

Just then Jeanette appeared in the doorway. "Well, what have we here? It looks like a family reunion." Jeanette turned to Lauren. "Aren't the babies wonderful?"

Dee and Melissa laughed. "Your mother's been asking everyone that. What can they possibly do but agree?"

"Well, they should agree," Jeanette said, "because it's true. I've got two adorable granddaughters. And maybe Lauren and Matt will complete the picture with a grandson in the not-so-distant future."

Lauren felt her neck tighten and she tried not to take offense at her mother's well-meaning comment. But the scene here was beginning to wear on her. Her sisters-in-law looked so happy. Motherhood glowed on their faces. With her own sad state of affairs, she found it hard to take.

"Well, I really have to get to the office. I've been out all morning and haven't checked in with Casey." She smiled at Dee and Melissa. "I'll be coming by daily to check on those babies. I can't wait until you get them home so I can spoil them. Bye now. Bye, Mother."

Lauren beat a hasty path toward the elevator. So much for bravado. She felt drained—and very melancholy. How long would she be able to keep up this act, she wondered, this pretense of her marriage being normal?

The rain had slowed to a fine drizzle as Lauren hurried toward the car. The air was still warm, so Lauren turned on the air conditioner in her car. Her cotton shirtwaist was slightly damp from the rain and the mixture of wet clothes and refrigerated air chilled her body. She sneezed. All she needed now was pneumonia to complete the picture.

Casey was just ahead of her when she pulled into the office parking lot. Lauren tapped the horn and gave Casey a little wave. Casey made a mad dash through the drizzle with Lauren following close behind.

"Hi," Casey said. "Aren't you a little behind schedule today?"

"A little. I had to stop by and see the latest additions to the family. Two young ladies."

"Both girls!" Casey exclaimed. "When did this happen?"

"Late last night and very early this morning."

"Moms and daughters okay?"

Lauren nodded.

"I'll have to go see everyone this afternoon. How does it feel to be an aunt?" She pushed open the door of the office, and Lauren followed her in.

"Pretty nice, I think. I'm still getting used to the idea of two nieces. I can't wait to hold them."

"That'll be good practice for you for later on—when you're cuddling your own little bundle."

Lauren froze, then the tears she'd been holding back all morning began to flow.

"Lauren, what's the matter?" Casey, her eyes like saucers, stared at her friend. "Whatever did I say?"

"Oh . . ." Lauren couldn't go on. She could feel her lower lip quivering. She felt like such a fool—in every sense. "It's not you—it's me, and Matt. Things are so rotten between us."

"I knew it. I was sure something was wrong last night, and you just wouldn't talk about it." Casey fished in her purse for a tissue and handed it to Lauren. "This Phoenix Center crisis has been real hard on Matt. Everything will probably go back to normal when he gets it resolved."

"No, it won't." Lauren began describing the situation to Casey, telling her why Matt had been so anxious to get married. About his reaction when Lauren told him she'd discovered the truth. "I feel like I'm walking on eggs and they're all cracking under my feet."

"So what are you going to do about it?"

"What *can* I do? If it were just business, then I'd accept the fact I'd made a deal and bail him out. But it's become more than that for me. Your stupid friend here has fallen for the guy."

Casey smiled. "Then everything's going to be fine. At the risk of having my head bitten off again—Matt loves you, Lauren."

"You don't know what you're talking about."

"I think I do. You two are so right for each other—you belong together. If only you weren't so defensive about the Grayson money."

"That's ridiculous," Lauren snapped.

"No, my friend, that's the truth. With women it never mattered—you never worried about what they wanted from you. But with men, it was different. You've always been overly suspicious of their motives."

"I have not." Lauren didn't like what she was hearing. Admittedly she'd been careful about men. Experience had taught her to be. It just made good sense. But being cautious and being paranoid were two very different things. Casey was mistaken.

"You have, and you are," Casey argued. "Ask anybody. Ask your father. That's a good idea—ask your father. Ask him about Matt. Find out the truth and quit jumping to conclusions."

"AND JUST HOW did you happen to decide Matt married you only for our connections and our money?" Lyle was glaring at her across his desk. Lauren looked away, her eyes resting on the bronze sculpture of a horse and rider on the credenza. She didn't want to look at her father. His expression wasn't pleasant. "Did he tell you that?"

"Not in so many words. But he didn't have to." Lauren wasn't sure what to say now. How could she explain to her father about placing the ad? Lyle would never understand why anyone would advertise for a husband. He was an old-fashioned, conventional man. But she had little choice, so she told him the whole story.

"So you see, Daddy, it isn't as though we married for love. It seemed like a reasonable thing to do at the time. Matt thought it was crazy at first, and then he found out I was your daughter. That apparently made me much more desirable. So it doesn't take a lot of brains to put two and two together. I know he needs financial backing to save his precious Phoenix Center."

Lyle stood up, then sat back down, clearly shaken by what she'd told him. "Sometimes two and two add up to five. Did he ask you for money?"

"No. Why should he ask me when he could go to his banker father-in-law?"

"So you think Matt's getting the money he needs from me?"

"Or maybe L.J. or Roger. This morning Melissa said Matt's getting things straightened out."

"And what does your husband say?"

"Nothing." A tear rolled down Lauren's cheek. She quickly wiped it away. She was feeling more upset by the minute. She really hadn't expected her father to be so annoyed with her. But then, he probably had a right, she decided, what with learning about the stupid advertisement and the way she'd got herself into this mess. "To tell you the truth, Matt and I don't say very much to each other anymore."

"Obviously." Lyle shook his head in exasperation. "Lauren, meeting a husband through the want ads may be a little offbeat. I know it is to me, anyway—but I get the strong impression there's a great deal more emotion involved now. Am I right?"

Lauren nodded, her head bent to avoid her father's gaze.

"I happen to think Matt loves you."

Lauren's head jerked up. "You're wrong—" Lyle raised a hand to stop her.

"I don't think so. Honey, you need to understand something. All marriages are partnerships to a certain extent. But they need other elements to survive. They need love and trust."

"But the television news and all the papers keep referring to Grayson money."

"You believe them over your husband?"

"Matt hasn't denied it."

"Why should he have to? In my opinion, Matt is a tough, honest businessman and a hell of a lawyer. Not some cad who'd resort to 'petticoat financing.' You know why I'm positive Matt Kennerly loves you?"

"No."

"Because I offered to help him raise the money he needed for Phoenix Center and he wouldn't accept my help. He said if he did it might jeopardize your relationship. So the question is whether you trust your own husband. Do you?"

She hesitated.

"Well do you?"

"I want to."

"Then it's high time you acted like it." Lyle came over and put his arm around his daughter. "Princess, I always worried about your notion that every man you met was more interested in my bank account than in your numerous charms." He dropped his arm and moved away a few inches. "You waited a lot longer to marry than your mother and I would have liked, ruling out every eligible male in sight. Then Matt came into your life. It was like the answer to our prayers. Forget the unorthodox way you came together. Concentrate on the future."

"But why didn't Matt just tell me I was wrong about him?"

"He probably resented your accusations. I would have."

"If he's out of the woods on Phoenix Center, like you say, then where did the money come from?"

"Is it that important?"

Lauren nodded. "I need to know, Daddy."

"Matt's got a lot of friends in Dallas. One of them arranged a buy-out by a Canadian firm. Okay? Now, what are you going to do about your marriage?"

Lauren didn't have an answer. Her father hugged her, his embrace softening his earlier criticism. She looked up at him. "Any ideas for mending fences?"

"Your mother and I have a system that works beautifully." He laughed. "It's called eating crow. Best method I know for ending an argument."

Lauren had no opportunity to take her father's advice that evening, because Matt again chose not to come home. She waited up until two hoping he would arrive, but finally gave up. She was tempted to call his old apartment to see if he was there, but her pride stood in the way. How could she deal with him if he wasn't willing to meet her halfway? Still, she couldn't help wondering where Matt was spending his nights... and whether he was spending them alone.

"WELL, GOOD MORNING. Are you feeling better today?" Casey was bubbling as usual. Sometimes Lauren wished the fizz would go out of Casey's personality. She felt miserable—she'd had only two or three hours sleep at best—and the last thing she was up to dealing with this morning was a perky partner. Alas, Casey was at her perkiest. "Well?"

"No, I'm not feeling better, thank you."

"I'm sorry to hear that. I was hoping the problem had resolved itself."

Lauren stared at her partner. "Surely you're joking. Matt and I don't have a problem that can be settled overnight."

"Are you sure it couldn't be resolved—especially overnight?" Casey raised one eyebrow.

"Matt and I didn't have a little spat over which movie to go see—we had a major falling-out. I was all ready to grovel after talking to you and Daddy, but I didn't get a chance. Matt didn't bother to come home. So, if anything, our marriage has deteriorated since we last talked." Lauren sifted through the mail on the desk hoping to thwart Casey's efforts at conversation. She failed.

"Okay, so last night didn't work out. That doesn't mean all is lost. Maybe Matt's staying away just proves how upset he is and how much he cares. Why don't you call him and find out?"

"No way." Lauren's eyes narrowed. She felt her hackles rising. "If he wants to behave like a mature adult and come home, then I'll apologize. But I'm not chasing him all over town to beg his forgiveness."

"Then you're crazy. If ever I saw a man worth begging to, it's Matt Kennerly. And from what you indicate about his degree of anger, it's probably going to take more than a simple apology to get him back. I think what we need is an all-out plan of action...."

"WHAT'S THE OLD SAYING—'a day late and a dollar short'?" Lauren watched nervously from the couch as Matt paced his office, each footstep making a new imprint in the plush carpet. She'd decided to try to make amends, offer him an apology of sorts—though her plan of action was backfiring. Periodically he would slap the folded papers across his palm. Finally he spoke. "I suspect you know damn well I don't need your precious money."

"I know you've worked out something for Phoenix Center—or so I've heard." Lauren realized her logic might be a little farfetched, but she'd hoped that offering her assets to Matt as collateral would be taken as an olive branch. She wanted him to know she trusted him— that what was hers was his. Unfortunately Matt didn't appear to be in a peace-making mood. "But I thought there might be other problems I could help with. You've confided so little about your business affairs...."

Matt stopped pacing and glared her way. "A fact you've mentioned on more than one occasion." He went around to his desk and took a seat, unfolding the documents and attempting to rub out the creases as he quickly scanned the contents again. Lauren saw his brows meet as he glanced over the papers she had brought—her financial statement, the deed to her office building, a release that allowed Matt to access funds from her trust. "Whew—no wonder you suggested a prenuptial agreement. This is a tidy little sum."

"My grandparents left each of the three of us a separate trust fund. I've had little occasion to use any of mine, so it's just been reinvested."

"And the building?"

"A gift from Daddy."

"Lucky girl. Rich parents and rich grandparents. Not just born with a silver spoon, but a whole damn place setting. Some of us weren't so fortunate. We were born poor and had to work for a living."

"I work!" Lauren protested, rising to her feet. Besides..." She gestured with her hands as her eyes took in the luxurious office. The elegant surroundings were proof Matt wasn't some young struggling attorney, even if he had been caught in a brief financial jam.

"I'll admit I do all right, but I'm not even close to being in your league." He re-opened the deed, which had folded over itself and started reading. "I can't believe your mother referred to this as 'Lauren's little business.' Classic Interiors—just a 'little business' that is the principal tenant of a little high rise on Turtle Creek, a high rise owned by Lauren C. Grayson. Not exactly a low-rent district, would you say?" He refolded the paper. "But what does Casey think about your offering the building housing your business as collateral for me to use?"

"Legally Casey has nothing to say about the property, since Classic Interiors gets the space rent-free. On a personal note, however, she was all for it."

His eyebrows raised.

"Matt—you might as well know. Casey is the one who set us up. The one who sent me your business card. She's responsible for us getting together in the first place, so I suppose she feels partly to blame for our problems."

"So that's who it was. I'm surprised. Are you sure it was just Casey?"

"What are you insinuating? That I contrived our meeting?" She stood over Matt's desk glowering at him. "You flatter yourself." Lauren reached for the papers. "Since you don't need these..."

Matt pulled the materials back out of her reach. "Now hold on just a minute. I said I didn't need money for Phoenix Center. But this is very interesting information. I think I'll hang on to these documents for a while."

Lauren knew he was goading her, trying to get an angry reaction. Obviously he felt he deserved redress for her false accusations—and perhaps he did.

He tucked the papers under the blotter. "I must admit my...business arrangements haven't exactly been rousing success stories of late. But now that Phoenix Center's taken care of, I may want to make another business deal." He leaned back in the chair, his hands stretched behind his head. "I'll get back to you."

That did it. Lauren walked over to the couch for her purse. She'd put up with his being difficult. She'd even made a valiant effort to get back in his good graces, allowing her pride to slip more than a bit, but Matt was going too far. No way would she completely abandon her self-respect. She still had some backbone. "Well I hope you've had a good time this morning. I came here to try to make amends, but I can see you have no intention of letting me do that. So, okay. Just sit there like a spiteful kid and enjoy yourself. But don't expect me to endure another second of it. You've had your fun. Now it's over." She stalked to the door. "Goodbye and good riddance."

"YOU AND YOUR ROTTEN IDEAS, all of them!" Lauren muttered under her breath to Casey as she entered the office, a brief hello and a phony smile pasted on her lips for the customer seated there, and a murderous look for her partner. She walked tensely toward her office, took a seat at her desk and began fidgeting. She worked on straightening a paper clip, then flipped it on the desk and picked up a pen, doodling feverishly on the paper in front of her. She hated being this angry. Right now she wished there was a punching bag in her office. One with Matt's face painted on it. The intercom rang.

"Matt's on the phone, Lauren."

"Thanks, Emily." She pressed down the blinking button.

"Yes." She hoped the ice in her voice had the proper chilling effect.

"Look, I acted badly a while ago."

"Stop the presses. This is real news."

"Will you just can the sarcasm for a minute and let me finish?"

Lauren didn't respond.

"I had reason to be good and mad. You put our marriage on the skids—first by accusing me of being the latest version of the American gigolo, then coming over to make amends by throwing guilt money at me." He sighed loudly. "At first I thought it was a setup—you out to prove you were right all along. Then I realized that you were operating in the only way you know how. No wonder you wanted a business marriage. That was the kind you felt secure with."

"Are you through?"

"Almost. I just wanted to say that I have no intention of touching a dime of your money. Thanks, but no thanks." He hung up.

Lauren slammed the phone down. Well, that call sure made her feel better. She now wished for two punching bags. One for each hand. She looked up to see Casey enter the room.

"So what were you snarling about when you came in? Things didn't go too well with Matt?"

"You might say that." Lauren related the office visit and subsequent phone call. "That was the worst idea you've had yet."

"Now hold on a moment." Casey plopped herself down in the chair opposite Lauren's desk. "That part was your idea, not mine. I talked about making amends—you're the one who wanted to make financial amends, and I just went along with it."

"You should have stopped me. Matt, and Daddy, too, have this big thing about trust. All I wanted to do was show Matt I trusted him—with everything. It seems I'm fighting a hopeless battle. No matter what I do, I lose."

"You just need to use the right ammunition."

"Oh? Like what?"

"Like something more personal, more romantic. Something of yourself."

"Forget it. I've had enough abuse from Mr. Kennerly, thank you."

Casey laughed. "Who do you think you're fooling? You know you want that man back—you've just got to find a way to get to him, to his heart."

"How about with a knife?"

"Come on, no joking. We've got to come up with another strategy."

"WHY DO I LISTEN to Casey?" Lauren groaned as she lugged the last of the grocery bags into the house. She dropped the two bags onto the counter and slipped off her shoes. Where was that cookbook? Ah, over on the table, the sales receipt marking the page for the entree she'd chosen to make for dinner that night. She flipped through the book again. The recipes looked as complicated as before—almost eight hundred of them. Well, all she had to cook was one.

She turned to the marked page. Chicken Marsala—that was one of her mother's favorites. "'The way to a man's heart is through his stomach'—don't forget that old saying," Casey had instructed. It had sounded like a good idea. And Lauren was desperate for good ideas.

Hat figuratively in hand, she called Matt again. "You were right," she said. "That was a heavy-handed approach I took earlier and I shouldn't have done it. It was misguided—a poor excuse for an apology. I'm sorry."

"Okay," he replied laconically.

"Are you coming home tonight?"

"Why do you want to know?"

"I thought I'd cook dinner for us."

"Hmm."

Lauren could just picture Matt's smirk.

"I'll be there," he said. "I sure as hell don't want to miss this once-in-a-lifetime event." The phone clicked in her ear.

"That was a gracious acceptance," she said into the dead phone. She had half a mind to call him back and tell him what he could do with his condescending attitude. But she meekly replaced the receiver as she recalled her father's advice about eating crow, and went back to her chores.

She filled the refrigerator and pantry with her purchases, then went upstairs for a quick shower, and changed into clothes more suitable for cooking than her black silk suit. Returning to the kitchen, she pulled out the new skillet, the package of chicken breasts, and the rest of the ingredients for the meal. "This isn't so bad," she told herself, holding up her new apron.

She'd never owned an apron before, but Casey agreed it would add the right touch. "At least you'll look like a cook." She slipped the apron over her head and tied the sash. Now she was ready to begin.

"'Pound each chicken breast-half with a meat mallet or the dull edge of a French knife,'" she read aloud, wondering what a meat mallet looked like. She didn't think she had one. Lauren rummaged through the cutlery drawer—there were only six utensils, the ones that came with a set she'd purchased when she moved in. Nothing looked like a meat mallet, and the knives all had sharp edges. "Improvise," she told herself. "All good cooks improvise. Mother does." She went to the garage and retrieved a hammer from a tool chest in the corner. It would work. All she had to do was clean it up a bit.

She was washing the hammer when Matt came in the back door. "This looks interesting," he drawled.

"You're home." That was a bright observation, Lauren thought. Nothing like a clever wife to keep a man at her beck and call.

"I couldn't resist—been thinking about it ever since you called." He looked over her shoulder as she began pounding the chicken with the hammer. "The thought of you cooking dinner was an intriguing notion if I ever heard one. This I had to see."

What was the big deal? Did he think she wasn't up to a simple meal? She'd never cooked because she'd never wanted to cook. She could be as domestic as the next person if she just put her mind to it. "There's some champagne in the fridge. Why don't you open it for us?"

"Well, you've sure pulled out all the stops."

Matt seemed amused, but Lauren didn't mind. She'd much rather he be amused than angry. She could deal with his smart-aleck tendencies much more easily than with his wrath. "Thought we'd better celebrate. Like you said earlier, this is a once-in-a-lifetime event."

"That's too bad. Maybe I should have rented a video camera, preserve the moment for posterity." He picked up the cookbook. "Need any help?"

"Maybe later," she hedged, wanting to get him out of the kitchen. He made her nervous. "Why don't you go change."

"Into something more comfortable, you mean?"

Lauren ignored him and returned to her cooking.

"You forgot to dip it in the egg first. I don't think the breadcrumbs will stick." Matt was sitting on the cabinet, wearing a pair of old faded jeans and a torn T-shirt, his feet bare. His wardrobe change was irritating. He looked as if he were ready to clean out the garage. So much for a "let's make amends" evening. And his suggestions were not helping, either.

"Did you use butter or margarine? There's a lot of cholesterol in butter."

She dropped a piece of chicken into the beaten egg mixture, then turned to the sink and rinsed off her hands. "Do you want to do this?"

He put his hands up. "No, no. You're the cook."

"If you feel an overwhelming need to be in charge, I'll gladly relinquish the kitchen duties to you."

"Sorry, didn't mean to take over." He gave her a tight grin. "But you've never made any secret about your cooking abilities—or rather your lack of them." He picked up the hammer and started toying with it. "I was just trying to help."

"So help by reading the newspaper or by watching the evening news or something."

"I haven't been too crazy about the news lately. Ever since I became part of it."

Lauren sighed. She'd hoped to avoid any unpleasantness for a few hours, but she'd known it wouldn't be easy. Clearly it would take more than a few feeble efforts at domesticity to sway Matt's thoughts from the real problems between them. "Matt..." she started to apologize again, the apology she'd begun that afternoon on the phone. But she stopped. It wouldn't do any good anyway. He'd never be willing to forgive and forget. She walked to the refrigerator and pulled out a plastic bag of green beans. "Now where is that cookbook?"

"What are you making now?"

"Green beans. We're also having scalloped potatoes." That ought to please him, she thought smugly. Matt had once told her he loved scalloped potatoes, and green beans were his favorite vegetable. She washed the beans, then placed them on a board and began cutting them with a knife.

"You're supposed to use your fingers."

"What?"

"Don't use a knife. Break them apart with your fingers."

"Why?"

"I don't know why. Didn't you ever watch your mother snap beans?"

"Here. You do them." She dumped the board and beans on his lap. "I'll start the potatoes."

"You mean they aren't in the oven?"

"Hardly. I haven't fixed them yet."

"Good thing I had a big lunch. Scalloped potatoes have to bake for an hour. Looks like dinner's going to be late."

"What would I do without all this armchair quarter-backing? Thank goodness you're around to tell me everything I'm doing wrong."

"Well, I'm not going to stop now. Turn around."

"What?" She turned to the stove. "Oh, damn!" A heavy trail of smoke was rising from the skillet. The butter had turned a dark brown. The edges of the chicken were the same color. "Now look what you've made me do!"

"You mean you weren't making blackened chicken?" He laughed.

"Don't you laugh at me, Matt Kennerly." Suddenly the smoke alarm sounded, a loud ringing permeating the kitchen. "Oh, no. The security company will be sending the fire department."

"I'll call them. You just take care of... dinner." Matt was smiling as he moved to the telephone and began dialing the number of the security company written above it.

Lauren tried to shove the skillet from the burner, quickly pulling her hand away as the heat of the handle seared her skin. She grabbed a towel to protect her hand and pushed the skillet to a back, unlit burner.

Matt, just finishing his call, slammed down the telephone and grabbed her hand. He thrust it under the faucet and turned on the cold water tap. "Are you hurt?"

"Would you care?" she snapped.

"Of course I'd care." His eyes met hers. "I would care," he repeated. He took her hand from the water and moved it to his lips. "There. I've kissed it and made it well. Okay?"

"It's nothing. Not really a bad burn. The heat just surprised me." The same way the heat of his caresses surprised her, she thought. For a moment, she was speechless, then she looked back at the ruined dinner. "I think all's lost. Would you settle for a peanut-butter sandwich?''

"Let's eat out," he murmured. "I'll go change my clothes."

Lauren followed Matt to the stairs and called up after him. "Can we stop by the hospital afterward and take a peek at the babies?"

"Good idea," he yelled back. "I'd like to see those two young Grayson ladies."

Lauren began straightening up in the kitchen. She dumped the boneless chicken into the cat bowl. "Pandora, you're in for a big treat tonight." She was untying her apron when Matt returned.

"I'm ready to go," he said.

CHAPTER NINE

LAUREN MOVED DOWN the cafeteria line, sliding the plastic tray along in front of her. She pointed at a steamer tray of baked squash casserole to indicate her selection. "And peas, too, please," she said.

A cafeteria. He'd brought her to a cafeteria. She still couldn't believe it. Was there some sort of subtle message being delivered? It wasn't as though Lauren disliked the place. In truth, it was one of her favorite places to eat. The food was always good.

But she was hoping for more than a good meal that night—a romantic candlelit dinner and some amorous give and take. There was nothing romantic or amorous going on between them at all. The atmosphere was hardly appropriate.

After a couple of conversational false starts, she and Matt launched into some comfortable chitchat. The time together was surprisingly pleasant, considering the earlier disaster in the kitchen. Maybe it helped that they didn't broach the subjects of Wes, or Phoenix Center, or their marriage. But at least they talked.

Lauren wished they didn't have to operate at such a superficial level, wished that they were at a stage where they could hash over their problems. She'd had just enough psychology in college to know that the key to any relationship was communication—and they weren't really communicating. But maybe if they talked long enough, eventually they would start reaching one another.

They left for the hospital at last, and Lauren, lost in thought, was surprised to realize Matt was already easing the Mercedes into a vacant space in the hospital lot. He got out, then came around to help her from the car. "I saw your brothers at the club this afternoon. They were in high spirits about the babies."

"From the way they act you'd think Dee and Melissa were the first women to ever give birth. By the way—" the double glass doors of the hospital entrance opened automatically and they moved inside "—that was nice of you to send the flowers."

"I'm a nice guy, Lauren."

The rest of the Grayson family—Lyle, Jeanette, Roger, L.J. and the two new moms—were congregated at the nursery window on the fifth floor admiring the two tiny infants. After hellos and embraces, Lauren moved close to the glass to look at her nieces. Matt came up behind her and the two of them stood there staring wordlessly. *This could be us,* Lauren thought, *looking at our baby. But will that ever be? Will Matt come to understand that I love him?* She'd begun to hope again. He seemed to want to work things out too—maybe not as much as she did, but at least he was there. Surely that said something.

"The only thing missing is a husky little boy to complete the picture." Lyle Grayson was beside them, his arm going around Lauren.

"Aren't you rushing things a bit, Lyle?" Matt drawled. "We've only been married a little over six weeks."

"Okay. This time next year, then." Lyle smiled. His eyes darted to Lauren and he winked. She suppressed a groan. Did her father think relationships could be repaired this easily—that all it took was a couple of Band-Aids, a few hours of contrition, to end problems as serious as hers and Matt's? Probably. Lyle Grayson was a can-do person, a fixer, the type of man who was used to making things right for his family, and especially for his daughter. He was probably convinced his sage advice the day before had solved everything. "But remember, I want a grandson."

"We'll do our best, Daddy," Lauren replied, moving toward the elevator. She was thankful it arrived quickly, cutting off further conversation with her father. She heard him say, "Bye Matt, Princess. Glad you two are working things out," just as the elevator door closed.

Lauren didn't know what to say on the ride home. Being with Matt at the hospital, seeing the babies and her family, gave her renewed hope. Dared she think the two of them might work things out? Would that be unrealistic, wanting too much too soon? What was Matt thinking? He was very quiet. "Are you staying home tonight?" she ventured.

"Why do you want to know?"

She felt like screaming, "Because I'm your wife! Because I care about you!" The impulse controlled, she said, "You've been spending a lot of nights elsewhere lately."

"It hasn't been very pleasant at home."

"I realize that."

He turned his head toward her. "Are you asking where I've been?"

"I'm sorry," she said. "I forgot I don't have the right to question your whereabouts. That wasn't part of our agreement."

"That depends on whether you're simply curious, or whether you really care."

Lauren was silent.

"I've been at my apartment," he said evenly.

"I thought that might be the case."

"Well, now you know for sure."

"Matt, I *am* trying."

"I realize you are."

"Can't we talk about it?"

"Isn't that what we're doing?"

"You know what I mean."

"Lauren, I'm not in the mood for an unpleasant re-hashing of our difficulties. It's late and I'm tired."

"So we'll talk about something else—if I bring up a subject that's off-limits, then you just say so."

"I'm getting strong signals you want this marriage—this business arrangement—to continue."

Bravo for your power of deduction, she said to herself. Aloud she said, "You know I do."

He turned the car into the driveway and switched off the ignition. "Then it's going to be interesting to see how far you'll go to ensure that it does."

HE WAS AWAKE. She *knew* he was awake. Lauren was lying on her back staring at the ceiling, every now and then casting surreptitious glances Matt's way. He, too, was on his back, one arm flung over his eyes. Lauren reflected on the past few hours. There had finally been communication—not all pleasant—but communication nonetheless. They had talked, and that must count for something. Right now, however, she could do without talking and would happily settle for being held in his arms...

They'd also made love—or at least begun to. He'd started the moment they'd returned home, hurriedly, demandingly, stripping off her clothes and his own as they fell together upon the couch in the den. Then after arousing her body to a pitch never before reached, he'd inexplicably, suddenly, moved away.

It had been deliberate, calculated, she was sure. What was he trying to do? Well, it couldn't have been easy for him to turn away from her. Lauren knew now how much he desired her. She knew she pleased him. So whatever he'd done to her, and for whatever reason, he'd done it double to himself.

"I'm really tired," he'd said, as if trying to explain his actions. He grabbed his clothes and went up the stairs. When Lauren joined him in bed later, he had made no sound, but she knew he wasn't asleep.

"I'M GOING TO WIN him if it kills me," Lauren said to herself as she climbed the stairs the following morning, carefully attempting to avoid spilling any coffee out of the mug she was carrying to Matt. She approached the bed and set the mug on the night table.

Matt opened his eyes, catching her hovering over him. "What's going on?"

"I just thought you'd like coffee." She gestured toward the cup.

He sat up, rubbing his eyes as he reached for the steamy mug. "Instant?"

"No. I brewed it."

He moved the mug to his lips and grimaced as he took a sip. "You better stick to instant."

Do not respond to that, she told herself. *He's deliberately trying to test your patience. Remember this is a big crow you're working on.* "On that complimentary note," she said, "I think I'll take a shower."

Matt was still in bed when she came out of the shower. She removed the terry towel wrapped around her body and let it drop to the floor. Seductively, languidly, she dressed in lacy silk underwear, putting on a garter belt and sheer black stockings instead of her usual panty hose. It seemed to have little effect on Matt. He picked up a magazine to read as he drank his coffee. "Are you sleeping in?" she asked.

"No early appointments," he answered.

And not much sleep last night, she thought, whatever he pretended. "What time did you plan on getting home—so I can have supper ready. Yesterday was a fluke. Tonight I'm going to make a meal you'll never forget."

"Actually last night's was pretty unforgettable."

"Very funny. Let's just say you'll be pleasantly surprised."

"I'm sure," he said.

LAUREN TURNED THE DIAL to bake and slid the seafood quiche into the oven, then finished cutting up the fruit for a salad. Bananas, kiwi, cantaloupe, honeydew, watermelon, grapes—the combination looked appetizing. Even the poppy-seed dressing had turned out fine. "I knew I could do it. I just needed to be in the kitchen by myself with no one looking over my shoulder." She reached up and set the oven timer. "No burned dinner tonight."

Matt arrived at six, gave her a perfunctory peck on the cheek and headed upstairs for the bedroom. He came down fifteen minutes later, undressed, a towel clutched around his hips. He put his arms around her and gave her another kiss, this one more thorough. The towel between them slipped a little, but he grabbed it, then smiled. "Think you could run my car over to the service station and fill it up before dinner? I've got an appointment at eight and need a little time to go over some material before then." Assuming her response would be positive, he turned and went up the stairs.

Lauren gritted her teeth. Why didn't he get gasoline on the way home? She glanced at the oven timer. The quiche still needed another forty minutes. Oh, what the heck— she had time. She pulled Matt's key ring from the hook on the kitchen wall and headed for the car.

Matt had changed to slacks and a clean shirt and was sitting in front of the television set when she returned, a Scotch to his left on a nearby table. At least he could have set the table, Lauren grumbled to herself. He seemed to enjoy being catered to. Well, it'd better not go to his head. She wasn't sure how much longer she could keep up this act.

The timer went off and she opened the oven door to look at the quiche. The top was a dark golden brown. It must be ready.

The quiche tasted fine—what could be eaten of it, that is. The outer edges were firm, but the middle had only reached the consistency of thick soup. "I think you'd better give up this phony routine," Matt said. "I'm not sure my stomach and I can handle much more."

"It's not that bad—I notice you're eating it."

"Didn't have time for lunch, so I'd risk anything. Besides, I didn't want to hurt your feelings." He took his napkin from his lap and laid it on the table. "But this isn't necessary, Lauren. I didn't marry you for your cooking."

"Why did you marry me?"

"Not now, Lauren."

"When? I'd really like some answers."

Matt rose from his chair. "Then you're going to have to wait. At the moment, I've got a distraught client expecting me—he arrived home yesterday afternoon to an empty house. Wife, kids, furniture—all gone. I'm due over there now. Sorry I won't be able to help with the dishes." He grabbed his sports coat from the back of a chair and left.

MATT WAS STACKING a pile of clothing on the corner of the bed when Lauren came out of the shower the next morning—suits and shirts, a couple of ties, and a pair of jeans. "Are you going by the cleaners today? Could you drop these off?"

It was Wednesday, and he knew quite well she always went to the cleaners on Monday. Well, she wouldn't give him the satisfaction of thinking he was getting to her. "Anything for the man of the house." She secured the sash of her robe and went searching in her closet for something to wear.

"Oh, and by the way—" Matt came over to the closet "—could you possibly pick up a gift for my secretary? Her birthday is next week."

"Your secretary?"

"Yeah. She hates getting perfume all the time. Maybe you could think of something different."

"You bet." She smiled stiffly and turned back to her closet. "I will not let him get my goat," she said softly to herself. But as determined as she was, Matt was beginning to irritate her. It was good that he'd gone into the bathroom before she told him what she thought about buying presents for his employees. He didn't have his secretary do his gift buying. Why should his wife be asked to? She quickly dressed, then waved goodbye to Matt when he reappeared in the room.

"Okay, I'll see you tonight," he said.

"For a home-cooked dinner?"

"You're really going to try again?"

"Yes. I'll prove to you I can turn out a perfect meal."

"Okay, but not tonight—we'll have to make it tomorrow. I've got a dinner meeting this evening. Hey—" he pointed to the pile of clothing on the bed "—you forgot the cleaning."

Lauren returned to the room and picked up the clothes. Oh, how she'd love to throw them at him.

"WELL, HOW'S IT GOING? I hated being in that seminar this week—I twitched the whole time because I was dying to hear what had happened to you. So tell me, tell me." Casey was bubbling again. Lauren gritted her teeth.

"I'm beginning to like him about as much as I did that first day we met," Lauren snapped. "Do this, do that, bring this, bring that. This morning I had to drop his shoes off at the shoe shop, drop off his cleaning, and now I've got to call the dentist and cancel his appointment. All of a sudden I'm his personal maid and I'm not too happy with the part."

"What are you going to do about it?"

"I don't know. About the time I'm ready to explode, to tell him to go get himself another flunky, I look at him and see that's exactly what he's expecting, and I don't want to give him the satisfaction. I'll be damned if I'll give in to my emotions and let him get the upper hand."

"I hate to tell you this, but I think you already have."

"You're wrong. I'm approaching this coolly and reasonably. My feelings have nothing to do with it."

Much to Lauren's consternation, Casey started giggling. "I'm sorry. I just can't help myself. Lauren, if you weren't head over heels in love with Matt, you'd have told him to go fly a kite a long time ago. Instead you married the guy. It must be love."

"So I love him." Lauren dropped into one of the reception area chairs and sighed. "That doesn't mean my heart is ruling my head."

"You think the way you're acting now, playing the devoted little wife, is being intellectual—businesslike?"

"It was all your idea!"

"Now wait a minute. When I suggested a candlelight dinner, I meant one prepared by a caterer. You're the one who decided on the Ozzie-and-Harriet routine. The way you're carrying on I'm surprised you haven't started ironing Matt's underwear, scrubbing the floors and complaining about waxy buildup.''

''Oh, I don't intend to go that far. I am going to try dinner one more time, though. Of course, at the rate I'm going, I'll probably poison him.'' She smiled. ''Maybe that's not such a bad idea.''

''What are you doing now?''

Lauren had picked up a piece of paper and a pen. ''We never did get around to placing that ad for you,'' she answered. ''I'm tired of your living vicariously. We're going to find you a husband, and then we'll talk about your marriage instead of mine. Let's see now.... Red-headed sprite seeks energetic hubby...''

LET HIM FIND something wrong with this meal, Lauren thought, as she eased the cooked eggplant from the carton and placed it in a glass dish. The veal scallopini was already simmering in a baking pan in the oven, and the pasta salad had been transferred to a bowl in the refrigerator. Lauren gathered the white cartons from the countertop, threw them into the trash compactor, then thought better of it. She grabbed a green garbage bag from the drawer, dumped the cartons into it, sealed the bag with a twist tie and carried the bag outside. The evidence had now been removed.

So she was fudging a little bit, so what? She'd cut up the carrot and celery sticks, hadn't she? Did it really matter that most of the meal had come from an Italian takeout? In this case the end justified the means. She had to prove she could put one decent meal on the table. And where had she heard that you didn't have to know how to cook, you just had to know people who could? Besides, she was trying to win her husband back. All the stops were out. She decided to quit wasting her time trying to cook and to turn her attention elsewhere. She was going upstairs to get gorgeous and sexy. Let Matt Kennerly try to resist this double treat. He didn't have a chance. Lauren smiled contentedly as she climbed the stairs.

Matt arrived home about six, surprised that dinner was on the table. "I don't know how you did it," he said a short while later, "but that supper was wonderful." He took another swallow of wine. "Did you really do it all yourself?"

Lauren crossed her fingers under the table. "Do you see a cook or a maid anywhere?"

"Sorry—didn't mean to offend." He leaned back in his chair. "I guess now is a good time for some meaningful conversation. This meal was just setting the stage. Right?"

"Not necessarily." Lauren got up and moved behind Matt's chair and wrapped her arms around his neck. "We don't have to talk at all. Unless you wanted to talk?" she asked, nipping his ear with her teeth.

"Talk? No, not particularly..." He rose and took her hand to lead her upstairs.

Lauren paused on the landing, looking at him with her fluid brown eyes. "Does this mean you've finally forgiven me—that we can start all over?"

"I forgave you a long time ago, babe. Or hadn't you noticed?"

"Was that your way of forgiving? Seemed to me more like you were just enjoying giving me a hard time."

"I enjoy... giving you a—"

Lauren's hands over his lips silenced the words. "Couldn't prove it by me." She smiled.

"Couldn't?" His arms folded around her in a tight embrace, as his lips covered hers, closing off the very breath of air. His fingers found the buttons of her blouse and, without letting go of his hold on her, somehow he managed to dispose of their clothing.

Matt pulled away, and his hands stroked her nude body. "I love the way your body responds to mine...love the way it makes me feel." Hands entwined they moved to the bedroom.

Hours later they lay together, only partially sated by their lovemaking. He turned to kiss her again, but was halted by the ring of the telephone.

"No problem, Lyle, we weren't asleep." Matt's eyes, teasing, went to Lauren's. He moved his hand to rest on her stomach, then after a few minutes of conversation, she felt his body tense. He sat up. "Oh, is that right? You did? Yes, she can be anxious sometimes." He looked at Lauren, his eyes cold.

Now what was wrong? Was it something her father had said?

"I don't think we can make it, Lyle." Matt's voice had a strained sound to it. "I've got a busy week. Thanks, anyway." He hung up the phone and rose from the bed.

"What was that all about?"

Matt didn't answer. Instead he moved to the landing, returned with his clothes and started dressing.

"Matt, what's the matter? What's happened?"

"Your father just told me about your Phoenix Center discussion. It's nice to know Daddy clarified my financial arrangements to your satisfaction. Him, you believed. Me, your own husband, you wouldn't." He turned around to face her. "I didn't think a little trust was too much to ask. Just a little trust, Lauren."

"You're a fine one to talk about trust," Lauren snapped. "If you'd trusted me in the first place and told me what was going on, I wouldn't have had to find out the details from my father."

"How could I tell you? You'd have run straight to Daddy so he could fix everything, and how would that have made me look? Your father would have tagged me as a real loser, using my wife to front for me."

"A lot you know. First, I don't generally run to Daddy with my problems. I'm a big girl—I can take care of myself. Second, my father would never think ill of you."

"Oh, no? I don't think Lyle Grayson would appreciate his daughter being married to a businessman on the skids. He would have been very concerned for you. His precious little girl. His princess."

"You don't know what you're talking about!"

"The hell I don't. The signs were there from the beginning. I'm surprised you had to advertise for a husband. Couldn't Daddy find one to your liking? Why didn't I listen better? A stupid mistake for a lawyer, a fatal mistake for a husband."

He grabbed a duffel bag from the closet and started throwing in underwear and socks. "I was a fool to think you were ready to be a wife—to believe all that garbage about your wanting a home and family."

"But that's what I do want—you were the one who wouldn't give it a chance, always at the office, always avoiding a real commitment. I don't know what all Daddy said, but that's beside the point now."

"I don't think so. I think it's exactly the point. You said not too long ago your vision was clear. Well, so is mine. You were only willing to believe me about Phoenix Center when Daddy said it was okay, to support me when he gave the green light. I'm sorry, Lauren, I thought I was marrying you, not Lyle Grayson. Lyle is a fine person, but I thought we would be a couple, not a trio. I need some time to think, some time away from you." He grabbed the bag, stormed out of the bedroom, and out of the house.

"My FATHER CALLED and apparently spilled the beans about my checking with him on Matt." Lauren sobbed. "Matt went into a rage." She was sitting in her den in a terry bathrobe. It was three o'clock in the morning. Casey was with her, plying her with hot tea and sympathy, but neither was doing any good. "I love him and I don't know what to do now...."

"And he loves you," Casey comforted. "I'm sure of that. Matt wouldn't have reacted so strongly if he didn't care. Can't you see where he's coming from, especially since your marriage was on pretty precarious ground anyway? You haven't been acting like yourself lately. You really went overboard trying to resurrect the marriage. He probably thinks you're just following Daddy's directions."

"But that's not so."

"How does he know?"

Lauren shrugged. "Any bright ideas for fixing this?"

"Naturally." Casey laughed. "Am I ever short of ideas?"

A MONTH WENT BY before Lauren, miserable, finally got up the courage to place a new advertisement in the *Dallas Sentinel*. She hadn't heard from Matt since the night he'd walked out, and following up on Casey's idea was a last resort. The ad read:

PARTNER WANTED: Abandoned wife wants another chance. Very specific qualifications—only dark handsome attorneys need apply. OBJECT: A long-term, very personal relationship.

Then she went to see Matt. She had conspired with his secretary to make an appointment for a new client—a Mrs. Smith. It was like a replay of their first meeting.

Lauren had stapled one of Matt's cards to the advertisement. She had even contemplated wearing the same pink linen suit, but decided it looked a little out of place on this fall day, so instead she opted for a navy gabardine coatdress. She just wished now that Matt would say something. He had been totally silent since she'd arrived, sitting statuelike behind his massive desk watching her. He certainly had poker-faced intimidation down to an art.

"I'm surprised you're here," he finally said.

"I almost didn't come."

"Actually I'm pleased by your tenacity."

Sure, thought Lauren, it must be a wonderful boost for his ego. She sat on the blue plaid couch, facing his desk. She was determined to maintain her composure and not let him intimidate her.

"So, why *are* you here?" Matt got up from his swivel chair and moved around to the front of the desk. He leaned back against the edge, stretching his legs in front of him.

She handed him the piece of paper and watched as he studied it. He must have known the kind of agony she was in as she waited for his response and he seemed to be drawing it out on purpose. Finally he raised his head and looked directly at her. "Will you answer one question?"

"What?"

"Do you love me?"

Lauren was stunned. She wasn't sure what she'd expected, but certainly not that. "Why do you ask?" She regretted her words immediately.

"That's not an answer."

"What difference does it make?"

"Why are you avoiding a response? It's a simple question, Lauren. Either you do or you don't. Do you love me?"

"Yes." Her voice was soft, barely above a whisper.

"Yes, what?"

"Yes, dammit, I love you!"

"That's all I needed to know." Matt pushed away from the desk and moved toward her. He held out a hand and she placed her hand in it, allowing her body to be pulled up against him. "And I love you," he said. "I've loved you from that first moment I walked out of my office and saw you waiting there in the reception area."

"You sure did a good job of hiding it." She smiled tentatively.

"That's because my reflexes were just too slow. I stupidly sent you away, and it's been hell to pay winning you over." His lips met hers in a long, hungry kiss. "I love you, Lauren."

"Then why did you walk out?" Her glazed brown eyes sought his.

"I wanted a real marriage—not a merger. But I wasn't sure you wanted the same thing." He sat down on the couch, pulling Lauren into his lap. "You never seemed able to forget about our agreement. To be able to trust me—to trust your own feelings. I had to leave that night. I was feeling diminished. And maybe it was a good thing I did go, because it gave me some time to think, to decide my stupid pride was getting in the way of our happiness."

He paused for a moment, took a deep breath, then went on, "When we decided to get married, I thought everything would be perfect. I'd seen so many rotten marriages, but ours was going to be different. We were equals—in almost every way. Then we'd no sooner said our vows than the problems with Phoenix Center came up. I hadn't had to worry about money since law school—but suddenly I had money troubles. How could I tell you—a woman who'd never had a financial problem in her whole life?'' Again he took a deep breath. ''In my mind, we were no longer equals.''

''You still should have told me.''

''I know that now. You were right. How could I expect you to have faith in me if I didn't confide in you? I forced you to rely on other people—mainly your father. I cut you out, refused to share my worries.''

''And would I have found out any of this if I hadn't forced the issue—if I hadn't come here today?''

''You'll probably never believe me, but I was just about to call you when I found out about the appointment with, er, Mrs. Smith.''

''Your secretary told you?''

''She was tired of the grouch I'd become. I think she realized what the problem was. Babe, I know I share the blame for what went wrong with our marriage. But I guess I wanted your love so much I was afraid to reveal any weaknesses.''

''But you must have known I loved you.''

''How could I? You never told me.''

''I was afraid to,'' she said. ''You weren't exactly shouting endearments at me, you know. I was frightened it would be one-sided—frightened you would never love me as much as I loved you. And you're right, I couldn't forget the agreement. After all, that was why we married.''

''No, that wasn't why we married, not why *I* married anyway. You listed a lot of reasons for a business arrangement—but our marriage was never that to me.'' He lifted her chin to stare into her eyes. ''I only had one reason for marrying you—I was head over heels in love. The kind of love I thought impossible until I met you. It really came to me on our wedding day when you appeared in that white bridal gown—I knew then I was a goner. Since then I haven't been able to give anything else the kind of attention I should have—it's a wonder I haven't become a complete washout in the courtroom. All the problems with Wes and Phoenix Center might have been avoided if I had been giving total attention to business rather than concentrating on my gorgeous wife."

"You could have fooled me."

"Apparently I did. We should have talked about it. Perhaps you can understand now why I avoided sharing—communicating. I was too vulnerable. I was afraid you wouldn't want to be my wife if you knew I loved you—that maybe you didn't want anything but a business arrangement."

"I want more—so much more. But I can't be just a fair-weather wife. You talk a lot about trust—well, it goes both ways. It means sharing, too, and taking the bad along with the good."

"I know that, now."

"I love you, Matt."

"Would you repeat that?" He dropped a gentle kiss on her ear.

"I love you."

"I'll never tire of hearing you say that. I love you, too. Expect to hear those words a lot."

"I need to hear them a lot."

"Considering the number of marriages that have been dealt a deathblow in this room, it's nice to know the place has been exorcised. Our marriage was born here. I adore you, Lauren."

"And I adore you."

"Of course, you realize marriage is a contract." His eyes took on a wicked glint. "Lots of business details to tend to. We'll need to make up a budget and so forth."

"I can handle that. After all—" she laughed "—we're going to have to free up some money for a cook."

"True. Plus, we may have another mouth to feed in the future, or maybe two, or three, or four more mouths...."

"Don't get carried away."

"Okay, only two or three. When you're making up that budget, babe, keep one thing in mind."

"What's that?"

"Just make sure there's no allowance for any more 'personal' ads," he said. "From now on, we do all our communicating—"

"In person," she finished for him. "I'm glad we agree."

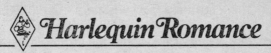
Harlequin Romance

Coming Next Month

Available in April wherever paperback books are sold, or through Harlequin Reader Service:

In the U.S.
901 Fuhrmann Blvd.
P.O. Box 1397
Buffalo, N.Y. 14240-1397

In Canada
P.O. Box 603
Fort Erie, Ontario
L2A 5X3

Harlequin Regency Romance™

Romance the way it was *always* meant to be!

The time is 1811, when a Regent Prince rules the empire. The place is London, the glittering capital where rakish dukes and dazzling debutantes scheme and flirt in a dangerously exciting game. Where marriage is the passport to wealth and power, yet every girl hopes secretly for love....

Welcome to Harlequin Regency Romance where reading is an adventure and romance is *not* just a thing of the past! Two delightful books a month, beginning May '89.

Available wherever Harlequin Books are sold.

Have You Ever Wondered If You Could Write A Harlequin Novel?

Here's great news—Harlequin is offering a series of cassette tapes to help you do just that. Written by Harlequin editors, these tapes give practical advice on how to make your characters—and your story—come alive. There's a tape for each contemporary romance series Harlequin publishes.

Mail order only

All sales final
